MASTERED: TEAGAN

SANCTUARY, TEXAS BOOK FOUR

KRYSTAL SHANNAN

Mastered: Teagan

Sanctuary, Texas Book 4

Copyright © 2015 KS Publishing

All rights reserved.

❀ Created with Vellum

PRAISE FOR KRYSTAL SHANNAN

"Wonderfully imaginative. Vampires have never been so sexy or dangerous." ~Liliana Hart, NYT Bestselling Author of the Rena Drake Series

"I couldn't put it down, action packed and sexy!" -Amazon Reviewer

"steamy love scenes, danger, friendship, magic, vampires, werewolves, adorable pixies and more!" -Amazon Reviewer

"Shannan weaves a sexy, action-packed tale sure to keep you turning the pages late into the night." ~~Liliana Hart, NYT Bestselling Author of the Rena Drake Series

"The dialogue is intelligent, exceptionally well written and flows effortlessly. Ah, the characters....they are the main component, the heart and soul of this story. Each and every character is fascinating, captivating, intriguing, engaging and sexy as sin." - Judy Lewis eagan walked through the open grand entrance of the Castle. She passed one of the largest men she'd ever met—one of the Blackmoor brothers, a Drakonae dragon-shifter—and into a spacious marble-floored foyer. Two grand staircases with wrought iron bannisters curled up to the second floor on either side of the space. That level of the fortress was the Blackmoor family's personal living space.

The majority of club activities took place on the lower level. There was a giant main hall with large cubicle spaces for scenes. Sitting areas for conversations and aftercare. Then there was the dungeon and the private playrooms, all named by color and each with its own personality to match.

A petite, pink-haired pixie greeted her. "Welcome to Luck of the Draw Night at the Castle, Teagan. I'm so glad you decided to give it a whirl."

Teagan smiled at Seely, the pixie who ran the Castle club and was second-in-command only to the twin Drakonae brothers, Miles and Eli, both dragon shifters.

"Seemed like a good change of pace. I don't like to get too attached."

Seely's eyebrow rose, a question tugging at her lips, but she didn't speak again. She merely gestured her forward, through the main hallway.

The Sisters, a group of special women with prophetic powers who lived in the castle with the Blackmoor dragons, usually mingled with out-of-town visitors, but tonight it was locals only and no Sisters allowed. It was a little strange, but everything about the town was different from the norm.

Luck of the Draw Night was supposed to be the best way to get matched up with a new Dom. Rumors that Fae dust played a role in the matching circulated through the town's gossip mill. She wasn't looking for any type of long-term commitment, but curiosity had won out over her normal antisocial behavior.

Teagan walked past several men from the pack in town. They ignored her, continuing to go on among themselves about the latest military news from the border. She didn't expect attention from them. She kept to herself in town and preferred to do the same in the club. The last thing she needed was some male thinking he could fix her. Or claim her.

All she needed was a Dom with a nice sadistic streak. Pain was her game. It had been since she'd lost everything she held dear in her life. If it weren't for the efforts of the Lycan Underground, she wouldn't even be alive. Sometimes she wondered if it would've been better that way.

She followed a couple of leather-clad women out into the garden courtyard.

"Welcome, friends. Please put your name in the hat. We will draw matches in ten minutes. Remember that just because you put your name in the hat doesn't mean you will be matched." A beautiful pixie with long, snow-white hair sat on a stool in the center of the courtyard. She held a black satin top hat and was clothed in a lacy merlot-colored dress that didn't leave anything to the viewer's imagination. She practically shimmered with magick, from her sparkling eyes to the ethereal glow of her skin beneath the red of the lace.

It wasn't a secret that Teagan frequented the Castle. Or that she chose to play with sadists who would make sure the only thing she focused on was the pain they inflicted instead of the pain she kept locked away in her mind.

She glanced around the courtyard, looking for her usual Dom, but Javier was nowhere to be found. The vampire was one of her favorite partners. He was willing to give her what she asked for. Lately though, he'd been avoiding her. So here she was, trying to find a replacement. She needed a Dom... a Master. The security of having someone else telling her what was going to happen, taking all those choices off her plate, was the only thing that kept her going right now.

Walking forward, she took a slip of paper and a pencil from the pixie. After writing her name on the paper, she folded it in half and dropped it into the hat.

The pixie smiled and took the pencil back from her. "Good luck tonight, Teagan."

Teagan smiled and stepped back from the center of the courtyard. Several tough-looking Doms were standing to her left. One of the particularly handsome ones smiled at her. His scent filtered across the open space—Lycan.

She moved away quickly, trying to put some distance between herself and the interested male. Lycans were bossy and territorial—she should know. An exclusive relationship was the last thing she needed right now. *That pixie better not match me with a wolf.* She hadn't met a Lycan Dom yet that liked to keep things un-exclusive.

She scanned the courtyard again.

Wolves.

They were all wolves.

No. This wasn't going to work. She shouldn't be here.

Teagan walked up to Kylie. "I'm sorry. I think I made a mistake coming tonight."

"You didn't. I promise." She laid a hand softly on Teagan's forearm. "If you decide you don't want the match, you can always say no before anything happens."

True.

And she really needed to let out some stress tonight.

Teagan took a deep breath and backed away. It was only one night. Anything could be survived for a night. It's not like she *had* to scene with whomever she was matched with. The pixie was right. She could always say no. The beautiful thing about BDSM clubs was the power she held over what happened each and every time she visited. Nothing would happen tonight unless she let it.

Unlike life, everything in the Castle was a choice. Nothing was forced.

This messed-up world had taken everything from her— friends, parents, her daughter, and her mate. The physical pain she sought was the only way she could release the torment she held inside her.

* * *

FINN WATCHED the skittery Lycan female try to back out of the hat drawing. He inhaled deeply, but she was downwind and he couldn't catch her scent. He'd heard her tell the pixie she'd made a mistake. But when Kylie told her she hadn't, his curiosity had been very piqued. That meant there was a good match for her here tonight.

4

He was here every Luck of the Draw Night Kylie hosted. He'd wanted a mate for years, but he wanted what his parents had. A fated match. He didn't want to settle for someone he couldn't have kids with. A lot of Lycans did, but he just couldn't bring himself to give up on that dream. If he could find her here at the Castle, all the better.

Ever since his cousin, Brogan, had introduced him to the lifestyle of D/s, he'd felt as though he'd found a piece of his soul that had been missing. He'd fallen into the scene at the club with ease and never had trouble finding a partner for an evening, but that wasn't what kept him coming back.

His goal was to find a woman his magick connected with. A Lycan female that needed to be cared for as much as he needed to care for her. The idea that a woman, his mate one day, would trust him so completely was what drove him forward.

She would appear.

One day.

Kylie was very particular about Luck of the Draw Night. The regular members of Castle knew this was the night you came to find a partner who complemented you perfectly. Fae dust was unlike any other magickal substance in the world. It could fulfill almost any wish of the pixie using it.

Kylie, the pixie holding the hat in the center of the court-yard, was one of the dungeon monitors who helped run the club for the Sisters and for the Blackmoor brothers. She was a sub, but a bratty one that required a Dom who enjoyed a little sass with his submission. It wasn't anything Finn was interested in right now.

The pixies oversaw and took care of the day-to-day activities and contracts between the Sisters and visitors so the Blackmoors could focus on their family and the protection of the town.

Kylie was also a fiercely strong sub whom he'd never had the pleasure to scene with, but he'd watched her with Miles and Eli in years past—long before Diana had returned. And even though he'd seen the dragons with other partners, they'd always kept things platonic. It was about the dominance for them. Not the sex. At least until their mate returned.

Kylie would make the right Dom one hell of a partner.

Right now he wanted to know more about one of the newer residents of Sanctuary. The Lycan female, Teagan, had been in Sanctuary a while but kept to herself. She was a frequent visitor to the Castle, usually with the vampire Protector Javier or a few of the other sadist regulars. He'd observed her scening with the vampire before and wasn't sold that she was really a masochist, but he wasn't her Dom and tried not to stick his nose where it hadn't been invited.

But tonight she looked available, and he was hungry. There was something about her. He just couldn't tear his eyes from her.

He'd asked around the neighborhood, but even the gossip queens didn't have much to tell him. Just that she kept to herself and hadn't shared her story with anyone since arriving in town.

Finn walked up to Kylie and dropped his name into the top hat.

The pixie smiled. "Glad you decided to put your lot in this evening."

"You know something I don't, sugar?"

Kylie raised an eyebrow teasingly. "You know I don't control the dust. We won't know until we know."

"Sure we won't. You feel matches before your dust picks them, and we all know it," he said, whispering the last part.

She laid her hand on his arm and then looked up, meeting

his gaze. Her blue irises sparkled with white flecks of magick, and he felt a chill rush along the skin of his arm, starting from where her fingertips touched.

"It's good you are in the drawing tonight, Finn. Though I'm surprised your own magick hasn't picked up on her yet." Her voice was matter-of-fact and gave nothing away. She was a hell of a poker player, and he hated that he couldn't get any kind of read from her response.

He grinned and nodded to her before walking back to his buddies standing to the side. Only one other of them had put his name in the hat tonight. Most of them were just going to wait around and pick up a sub that didn't get matched off... if there were any left.

Only five subs had shown up tonight. But if a perfect partner wasn't there that night, Kylie's dust wouldn't match them. Interestingly enough, he'd seen the dust not match certain people one night and then months later it would— like it knew exactly what those people needed at the time of the lot casting.

"Hey, man." Brogan jabbed him in the ribs and chuckled. "Which sub you got your eye on? Don't tell me it's the female who likes that vampire sadist. I saw you watching her."

He shot the male an angry glare. His wolf was pissed that Brogan was speaking disrespectfully about the little sub. It wasn't just his wolf that was pissed either.

"Shut it," he snapped, his fangs descending for a split second. *Damn.* His wolf was more upset than he'd thought. Surely Kylie couldn't feel a Lycan match before he did. His eyes searched the room again for a sign or scent of Teagan. Gods, he wanted it to be her.

Brogan threw up his hands in mock surrender. "Chill, bro. Didn't mean it that way. Masochists just aren't usually your drink of choice."

"We'll see soon enough," Liam added in, tipping his head toward Kylie.

Finn turned around, his eyes glued to the pixie's face.

Kylie placed her hand to the mouth of the top hat, and iridescent dust fell from her palm and into the hat with a soft white glow. She reached into the hat and pulled a piece of paper from inside. The dust had fused two names together.

"First match tonight is Lori and Cole."

A curvy brunette Lycan female near the main courtyard entrance beamed as the Lycan male he'd known several years crossed the space to escort her away. They disappeared down a long hallway, and Finn turned his attention back to Kylie's hand.

She reached into the hat again and brought out another match. The two fused pieces of paper glowed brightly in the moonlight shining down into the courtyard.

"There is only one other match for tonight." She took a breath and then read the names. "Teagan and Finn." Her voice was sure and unwavering.

He caught her bright gaze and she smiled broadly at him. The little twit had known the whole time. Sneaky little pixie.

Turning his head, he met Teagan's gaze and his stomach knotted. Her face read straight disappointment. Hold the doubt. She'd jumped straight to fear.

Why? She played with sadists. Why would a typical Dom make her look like she was ready to flee to the hills?

CHAPTER 2

*T*eagán sucked in a deep breath. That damn pixie had matched her with a Dom named Finn—whoever that was. And why were there only two matches? *What the hell?* She'd thought Luck of the Draw meant everyone got matched up randomly, not that they got matched up via magickal Fae dust! Those pixies at the market had a lot of explaining to do. *Meddlesome little faeries.*

The handsome Lycan who had smiled at her earlier was walking slowly toward her.

Nausea crept into the pit of her stomach. She just wanted a good beating. Was that too much to ask for? He looked—nice. There wasn't a hint of sadist anywhere in his demeanor. Finn's stare pierced straight into her like he was trying to get into her mind. Wolves could read human's minds without permission. But Lycan to Lycan only worked if both parties were open to it.

Not happening.

She didn't let anyone in, and she wasn't about to start for the approaching hunky Lycan Dom.

His brown eyes ate her up from head to foot, pausing a

few extra seconds on the top edge of her tight black leather camisole. A spark of warmth shot through her center, pleased that he found her attractive. It'd been a long time since she cared whether a male found her sexy... it was strange to feel pleasure from him noticing her now. She didn't want to care. Caring meant other feelings could follow, and she didn't want those feelings. As long as they didn't come, she would never hurt again.

She didn't deserve to ever feel happiness again. Bottoming for a sadist was the closest she could get to feeling enough pain to forget the overwhelming loss Fate had dealt her. It was the only way she could pay penance for failing her daughter and her mate.

He extended his hand as he approached. He didn't smile again, but his eyes were soft, as if he knew what a high flight risk she was. "I'm Finn. I'm looking forward to scening with you tonight. Do you know what you might want to do?"

His words were so formal, yet gentle. It took her completely by surprise. Talk about putting the ball in her court.

She slowly placed her hand in his large palm. "I'm Teagan," she returned, swallowing as his strong hand closed around her much smaller one.

His thumb stroked the top of her hand subtly, sending calming sensations through her tense body. Magick flowed back and forth between them and lit a spark deep inside her that she hadn't felt in decades. *It couldn't be possible.*

His eyes widened. He'd felt the magick too. His fingers tightened just slightly, holding her more firmly. "It's nice to meet you, Teagan. Walk with me." He gestured with his free hand to the long dark hallway that led to an open playroom outside the main club area.

She swallowed her nerves and nodded. It was just one

night. Right? She could handle any Dom for one night. Mate material or not. It didn't matter. He couldn't force the issue. It was against Lycan customs.

Maybe he was better with a flogger or whip than she assumed. She could ignore the warming sensation building in her core and just be a sub.

He dropped her hand, and she tensed again when he placed it instead at the small of her back. She stepped forward quickly, putting an extra step between them and breathed a little easier when his hand wasn't touching her any longer.

"Teagan, stop."

The command resonated deep in her heart. Without a thought, her feet stilled and she froze in place. Obeying Javier was a conscious effort. For this male she'd just— stopped. No hesitation.

"Tell me to go right now; otherwise, I don't want you to avoid my touch again."

"I'm worried you won't give me what I need," she said slowly, turning to face him.

"Why?" He stood patiently, his arms at his sides and his eyes studying her thoughtfully.

"You're not a sadist."

His lips curved slowly and his brown eyes darkened. The smoldering look heated her from the inside out. That look. The one he was giving her right now, was what she needed. The look that growled just-give-me-a-chance-to-make-you-regret-what-you-said. The look of a Dom ready to punish a sub. At least that's what she hoped he'd do.

"What are your hard limits, Teagan?"

She swallowed. "I don't have any. As long as it hurts, I'm fine with it."

His eyes narrowed, and his full lips straightened into a hard line.

She found herself wishing for another smile. Wishing she could touch his face and body and... *Oh, gods! What is happening to me?* The harsh glare she was getting from him now made her insides go cold. He wasn't scary in the I'm-gonna-hurt-you way, instead it was a scowl that made her feel disappointed in herself. The idea of disappointing him scared her more than Javier ever had with a whip or cane.

"Do you have a specific safe word?"

"Red," she answered. There had never been a need for anything more specific. She'd never had to safe-word out of a scene and didn't foresee it being a problem in the near future. No Dom had ever pushed her beyond what her pain tolerance could handle. There was no way this guy would either. He looked like he'd rather hug her than hit her.

No amount of physical pain could ever equal the emotional pain she carried with her every day. And physical pain was her only escape from the emotions. It didn't look like she was going to get much release tonight.

* * *

SHE WAS A MATCH. There was no denying the flow of magick between them. What he'd waited on for so many years had finally walked through the Castle door, but she didn't want him.

She wanted someone to hurt her.

No limits. She was a little further gone than he'd first assumed. Why was a sweet little thing like her looking for a sadist to torture her beautiful body? She was naturally submissive. He'd heard her breath hitch when he'd commanded her to stop. She'd responded without thinking.

She was perfect... except that he could tell something was off. The light that should've been in her eyes was dark. Not only did she desire pain, he would bet she lived with the memory of something terrible on her mind every day.

He did too. If she'd lost people, they shared that misfortune. When the shit hit the fan fifty years ago, his parents had gotten caught in the crossfire. Neighbors they'd lived next to for years had turned on them. His father had thrown himself in front of a bullet meant for his mother. When she'd crawled out from under her dead husband, the same neighbor had put a bullet in her head as well.

He and his brother had been running toward them, screaming for her to run. But she hadn't. When her body hit the ground with a sickening thud, they'd both changed.

They both regretted what they'd done next, but in the moment, revenge had been their only thought. The blood on their hands would follow them forever. The sounds of their neighbor's small children screaming from the porch still haunted his dreams some nights.

It was acts like those that perpetuated the hate, even though he and his brother hadn't started the fight. In those terrible moments, they had become the animals humans ranted about and feared.

Monsters.

He placed his hand on her lower back again. She flinched, but not nearly so noticeably this time. It was a shame that such a beautiful woman only wanted to feel pain. His touch made her uncomfortable, but he knew it wasn't personal. More than likely she didn't like anyone to touch her. At least not in a protective or gentle way.

The hallway forked, and he led her to the left, into one of the open rooms on the ground floor. Tonight they would stay outside the main club. She needed something different.

13

Her spirit was sad... broken. Even though she said she wanted to be put through the paces by a sadist, all he could see was a woman who needed to be loved. Treasured.

"We are playing in the courtyard room tonight."

"Yes, Sir."

She walked willingly beside him now, not attempting to break contact with his palm. The large garden room was mostly empty. Another couple sat in the far corner on a large, black leather couch. The Dom's face illustrated how well his sub was doing at giving him a blow job.

Finn walked Teagan straight to the opposite side of the room. "We will use the sawhorse tonight."

"Yes, Sir," she answered, a bit more energy in her voice this time.

"Go to the wall and choose two instruments," he commanded, gesturing to the wall to their right. All sorts of toys were displayed. Any type of flogger, paddle, whip, or vibrating toy was ready and available. If the Castle didn't have something a Dom or Domme desired, it was handmade by one of the local pixies. No one was allowed to bring anything inside the Castle.

It was a nice setup. Anything they used tonight would be removed from the room by an attendant, usually one of the Sisters, and sanitized or disposed of.

This patio room was cavernous, especially with the deep merlot paint on the walls and the ceiling. The lamplight was a soft yellow, mimicking candles on the walls. It was quieter here than down below in the main club area. Tonight he wanted it silent. He wanted to be able to hear her every breath and gasp.

A smile pulled at the corner of his mouth as he watched her run her hands over the selection of toys. He pursed his lips together to hide it. The cane she picked was thick—he'd have to be careful with that. The paddle was a sturdy leather one, about the size of a table tennis racket. She really did have it in her mind that he was going to beat her.

She returned and he took the toys from her, laying them on a small side table near the spanking sawhorse. This particular sawhorse had a padded top bar and padded arms for her elbows and larger ones for her knees, giving her good support but leaving her pussy and breasts nicely exposed. It also had a main lever for raising and lowering the height of the horse.

"Strip. Put your clothes on the table."

"Yes, Sir," she answered, bowing her head respectfully. She reached behind her back and tugged down the zipper for her leather top. Then she did the same with the short black leather miniskirt. She shimmied out of the skirt, revealing that she wore no panties.

Good girl.

She folded the skirt and laid it precisely on the table, then pulled the unzipped cami free from her breasts, letting them loose of their confines. They were gorgeous—round and full. Ready to be played with. She folded the leather cami, then stood tall and beautiful in nothing but her creamy white skin.

She was stunning.

He patted the bar and she leaned forward, lengthways, along it. She let her arms hang loosely while he adjusted the armrests to support her weight, then strapped her wrists down using the padded leather restraints attached to the sawhorse. Each time his fingers grazed her soft skin, he felt a surge. The magickal exchange between them was getting his wolf wound tighter than a cocked trigger on a Colt .45.

"How's your comfort level?"

"It's good, Sir."

15

Finn adjusted the height of the leg braces, then guided one leg and then the other into place until she was snugly secured. He patted the round globe of her ass, smacked first one cheek and then the other.

A surprised gasp slipped from her lips, and her scent changed instantly. *That wasn't magick. That was her responding to a light swat...*

Nothing hard and certainly nothing that a masochist would get off on, but it was a start for him. It was more to warm himself up to the idea that she was going to want him to hit her and cause physical pain. Using a paddle was fine, but her expectations with the cane were making him slightly uncomfortable.

He walked to her side, then slipped a hand beneath her stomach and the padded bar, indicating he wanted her to arch her back. She did, and he arranged her breasts to each side so that if she wanted to lean down on the bar it wouldn't hurt, plus he intended to attached some weighted clover clamps to her pretty pink nipples.

He picked up the rounded paddle from the table and began running it along her skin. Touching her shoulders, her back, her legs, and then finally moving toward her ass. He tapped lightly a few times and then struck each cheek once. A soft moan rolled from her chest. *Seriously?* He laid his hand against the reddened globe and rubbed, bringing more blood to the area.

"Count to ten."

"Yes, Sir," she answered.

He watched the muscles in her ass clench and release as she prepped for the strikes. Pulling his arm up, he brought it down in three successive pops.

"One, two, three," she called out, speeding toward the three like an old-fashioned cassette tape on fast-forward.

He slid his hand along the crack of her ass, letting his fingers slip between the folds of her pussy. She was already slick. A smile curved the corners of his lips as an idea bloomed in his mind. She claimed to be a masochist, but here she was swollen and drenched after a mere three strokes of a paddle. *Thank the gods.* Everything he'd been psyching himself up to do with her instantly changed course in his mind.

His dick hardened, but he dismissed his arousal. Tonight was about her. Only her.

He lifted the paddle and let it strike twice again.

"Four. Five," she moaned out.

Finn slid his fingers between her legs and spread her slick juices over her clit. She bucked against the touch but couldn't move more than an inch or two up and down or to the side.

"Ahhh."

He rubbed, alternating between putting pressure directly on her clit to circling the swollen bud. Then brought the paddle down a little harder on her pink ass.

"Six."

He turned his hand, facing the palm to the floor, and slipped a finger inside her pussy. Curling his finger downward, he smiled when she released an audible hiss followed by an all-over body shudder. She was close, but fighting it. *Why? Although, why would she claim to be a masochist and put herself through hours of torture without any pleasure?* She clearly was aroused.

"Come," he ordered, bringing down the paddle again while he continued to finger her with his other hand.

"Seveeeeeeeeeen." The number came out in a disappointed, languished voice. Like she was weeping over the orgasm.

Her vagina clamped down on his finger, and he could feel

the swells of her climax still rippling through her muscles even after she'd stopped panting.

"Good girl. That was a good start." He pulled his hand from between her legs and brought the paddle down three times in swift succession.

"Eight, nine, ten." She finished counting with a sigh, as if those last strikes had barely registered. "A start, Sir?"

He swatted her ass again for the question but bit back a smile, pleased she caught his inference even with her mind floating in the pleasure of her climax.

"I get to ask the questions, not you, sub."

"Yes, Sir. Sorry, Sir."

CHAPTER 3

*H*e'd only paddled her for ten counts, but already her body hummed. Already she'd climaxed. Usually she fought to find the place where she could release. The pain overwhelmed every sense when Javier whipped her. It wasn't uncommon for her to go an entire hour session and only come once.

She knew why her body responded so easily to Finn. But she didn't want it. She didn't deserve another chance at a life with a man, a family. A life where children could be a possibility again.

The magick was wrong. It had to be.

The pain in her nipples from the clamps had mixed into the general hum of everything else. Now, after the orgasm, she could barely feel the weights. He wasn't striking her though, so they hung still. Once the cane strikes started, they would jerk and yank on her swollen nipples.

She gasped as he slid another finger inside her wet vagina and rubbed gently against her front wall. A shiver ran through her, and she couldn't stifle the slight moan that escaped. It was strange to feel so much pleasure in one session.

She didn't deserve to feel this good.

I deserve pain.

That was why she came to the club. She craved the disconnect from herself. Only real pain allowed her to truly escape her memories. The exhaustion that came with being beaten. After Javier's sessions, she usually didn't get out of bed for several days while her body healed.

"Get out of your head, sub," he hissed, pulling his fingers out of her heat.

The air *whooshed* before she felt the sting of his palm connect with her ass. The burn surged through her like an inferno. She gasped in surprise as her body convulsed and another orgasm clamped down over her like a vise. She screamed, pulling at the cuffs as her muscles tightened and throbbed.

Again? He'd made her come twice in less than five minutes. She sucked in a breath and moaned as he massaged her bottom with his large hands. His fingers kneaded and rubbed, then slipped between her wet folds again. So slick. So wanting to have more than he was giving.

He walked to the table. She swallowed when she saw him pick up the cane. But then he put it back down and gave her a wicked smirk.

Her mouth went dry and she waited.

He walked over to the wall of toys and opened the top drawer of the black cabinet in the center of the wall.

Dildos?

Her ass clenched and she shivered. Anticipation of what he had planned drew beads of sweat to her forehead.

She craned her neck, trying to see what he was taking out

of the drawers. Several things clinked together, but his hands hid the items from view.

"We're going to fill you up a little before I play with the cane. Have you ever had a butt plug?" he asked, setting the toys on the table next to the cane.

"Yes, sir."

"Good." He picked up a large blue plug, a bottle of lube, and walked up behind her. She heard him squirt some liquid out of the bottle and then the cold gel hit the tiny ring of muscle between her cheeks. A small cry slipped from her mouth as he used the very tip of the dildo to work the lubricant inside her ass.

The tingle and warmth started almost immediately. She squirmed in her restraints and moaned, earning another sharp swat. She tensed, waiting for additional spanks, but they didn't come.

"Stay still." His voice oozed sex and control, and she wanted both. Craved both.

Since when, though? "Yes, Sir. Sorry, Sir."

"Good girl." He rubbed her burning ass cheek and then patted it affectionately.

She'd already come twice, and he wasn't showing any signs of stopping the session. He hadn't even used the cane yet.

She hissed as he slowly pushed and pulled the butt plug in and out, working it slowly past the tight rosebud of muscles. Her ass filled, and stretched and just a slight streak of delicious pain edged its way through her body. Her mind blanked, and she found the place where she didn't have to think. Didn't have to be herself anymore. Didn't have to remember everything she'd lost.

More pain was better. More pain made her forget. Made her feel a little less guilty for... surviving.

She breathed into a deep thrust and shuddered as her body clamped down on the toy. He patted her ass and moved toward the table once again. She watched him and released a sigh when he picked up the cane.

"You want this?" He held it up and ran the tip of it along her arm and over her shoulder.

"Yes, Sir."

Everything inside her wanted it. Wanted to escape from the pain in her head through the agony the cane could inflict. She'd already climaxed twice, maybe once more would be enough for him to feel like it was a successful scene.

A niggling feeling in the pit of her stomach said it probably wasn't going to be so easy.

He tapped the cane along the length of her back, building anticipation of a real strike.

Then he got to her backside and tapped the end of the dildo. Not hard, but just enough to stimulate all the nerve endings in the vicinity. She moaned and fought to remain still. He wanted her to be still. He'd already said it once, and swatted her when she'd moved. But the sensations running through her body from just the light tapping was bringing her up again.

She shivered as another orgasm began to curl and expand inside her. Muscles tensed. Her breath was already reduced to pants and gasps—when she remembered to take a breath at all.

"Please, Sir."

"Please what, sub? What do you want?"

"Harder," she gasped out.

He huffed. "I don't like my subs to bleed."

The cane came down with a whack on her ass, but the sting was nothing compared to what Javier doled out. She was accustomed to the bite of the cane or the fiery burn and sting of a whip. That was her whole reason for coming to the club. To escape from one pain into another. Her Lycan DNA prevented nearly any injury from creating a permanent scar. They never used enchanted weapons. Nothing in the club could truly hurt her, yet he held back—refused to give her what she wanted.

There was no point in continuing this session. She wanted to disappear. She didn't want to feel. Her safe word rose to her lips, but in the same instant she'd decided to call it quits, his fingers slipped deep into her pussy and she moaned as another orgasm surged forward.

A scream of pleasure tore from her lips instead, and she wrenched in the restraints as he pumped his fingers in and out of her vagina. She creamed over his hand, and she clamped hard around the dildo in her ass. His finger-fucking kept the orgasm rippling through her longer than normal, and by the time the last tremors slid from her body, she lay limp against the sawhorse, barely able to catch her breath.

She was vaguely aware of him moving about her, removing the dildo and cleaning her with a warm, wet wash-cloth. Probably dropped off by one of the Sisters or the dungeon monitors. It didn't matter. All that mattered was that he'd just given her the best orgasm she'd ever experienced and he hadn't beaten her.

It presented a problem she hadn't encountered before. On one hand, she wanted desperately to have those cherished moments where the world around her slipped away. When the pain from the beating was all she could focus on. When the consuming grief that stayed with her constantly wasn't the first thing on her mind everywhere she looked. Every small girl she saw. Every dark-haired man with his back turned, his hair cut like her sweet Ethan's had been. It'd been ten months since she lost them, and still she wanted to cry every moment of every day.

Tears began to run down her cheeks. There was no point in trying to hold them back. She hadn't felt pleasure like Finn had given her just now since... the last time she'd been with her husband, her mate. The man she was supposed to have spent her entire life with. It wasn't fair.

Being with Finn was a betrayal to her love for Ethan. To his memory.

"Red!" The sound of her voice calling out the safe word surprised her. "Red. Red." It just kept coming out. "Red!" It didn't sound like her. She didn't cry and wail. She didn't use safe words.

"It's okay, sweetheart. We're done." His voice crooned into her ear as his fingers flew to release the buckles holding her in place.

She heard a female voice ask if everything was all right, probably a monitor. Finn's low bass rumbled an answer that she'd come apart after the scene was completed. He told the woman he intended to hold her until she calmed.

Teagan couldn't see through her layers of hair, had no idea who had checked up on her, but it just showed the quality of the club. They watched everything to make sure everyone was safe.

A soft blanket covered her bare back, and Finn lifted her from the sawhorse. He cradled her as if she were no more than a babe and settled into the corner of a big couch a few feet away. He tucked the blanket around her tightly, giving her more of a sense of being covered. His scent filled her lungs, and she allowed her shivering body to lean against his chest. The soft *thump thump, thump thump* of his heart was calming.

Cold glass touched her lips and she opened her eyes. He was holding a cup of water to her mouth.

"Drink, sweetheart."

The water slid down her parched throat, and the shivers and sobs subsided until finally her breathing returned to normal.

He set the glass on a table behind her, and a whiff of sugar and cocoa caught her attention. He held a piece of chocolate between his fingers.

She licked her lips and nodded.

He pressed the candy into her mouth and she ate it slowly, allowing the sweet creamy chocolate to coat her tongue. She snuggled deeper against his chest and relaxed when his arms tightened around her.

"You did so well, Teagan. I'm proud of you. Thank you for accepting the scene with me this evening."

A sigh slipped from her chest as his kind words lulled her into a peaceful state. Her eyes drooped, then shot back open when his hard cock throbbed beneath her bottom. They hadn't had sex. He hadn't been able to reach his climax. She'd lost it. Used her safe word. Cried.

Javier never wanted sex, but another Dom would. *Wouldn't they?*

"I'm so sorry," she whimpered against his chest. Chancing a glance upward, her gaze met his and his eyes held only compassion. He wasn't upset. Angry. Or disappointed. In fact, he looked rather pleased with himself.

What the hell?

CHAPTER 4

*S*orry? Why was she apologizing?

"Teagan. Everything is fine." He smoothed her hair from her forehead and hugged her more firmly to his chest. Her soft body fit against his perfectly and he knew letting go of her was going to be a chore. If he had his way, he'd carry her out of the Castle and directly to his house.

"But you didn't. I didn't get you—"

"Shhhh. That wasn't what I wanted this evening. Tonight was just about you submitting and going where I told you to go."

She sighed something about his hard cock not being in agreement, and Finn was unable to hold back a grin. It certainly hadn't been easy to refrain from taking her pretty pussy when it had been practically weeping for him to enter her.

About an hour later she stirred in his lap. She was so beautiful and had slept so peacefully. The tension and fear he'd sensed in her earlier had faded in sleep, but as she woke it came back with a vengeance.

He released her and watched silently as she dressed in the cami and skirt she'd arrived in.

"Are your shoes in the foyer?"

She glanced to him and nodded. "Yes, sir."

"Did you walk or drive tonight?" The town was small. Lots of people had cars, but most walked, enjoying the atmosphere of quiet.

"I walked," she answered, zipping up her cami. "I apologize for falling asleep on you. I can't imagine how irritating that must've been, but thank you for letting me rest. I don't remember the last time I slept... so soundly."

"It was a pleasure. No irritation whatsoever," he said, rising from the couch. "I'll walk you home."

"I'll be fine," she said, turning away and starting for the door.

"Teagan, it wasn't a request."

She froze in the doorway and slowly twisted on her heel until her eyes flashed angrily.

There was more spark in them now than he'd seen yet.

"The scene is over. I respectfully request your release."

"Did you not enjoy my company?" he asked, keeping his voice firm but even.

"I do not wish more, if that's what you're angling for."

The sting of her sentiment was harsh, but he wasn't one to give up easily, especially when the woman turning him down was a potential mate. He'd waited this long to find someone he could have a family with. Fall in love with. Just because it was going to be more difficult than he'd hoped didn't mean he was going to give up on her.

"I'm walking you home. Nothing more than that."

She held his gaze for a moment before nodding. "Very well."

He walked at her side through the massive fortress to the

27

front foyer where she sifted through a large trunk for her shoes, and then out the open front door. Her footsteps were light on the sidewalk, but her heart betrayed her nerves, racing in tempo with the wild mustangs that used to run the open prairies of Texas decades ago.

"Why are you afraid of me?"

A quick catch in her breath said she'd heard him, but she didn't immediately respond.

Devising a lie, no doubt.

He smiled, waiting for her response.

"I'm not," she said.

Outright denial then. Brave girl.

They turned down a side street off Main Street Circle and followed the sidewalk into a neighborhood inhabited mostly by the Lycans Travis and Garrett had brought back from the Washington Republic.

"I'd like to scene again. When can we meet?"

She stopped in front of a small white house with blue trim and faced him squarely. "I'm not sure we should."

"I'm quite sure we need to," he replied, not missing a beat. She wasn't going to get out of it that easily. She could try to hold out, but eventually the call of their wolves would dominate her every waking thought.

Unless she flat-out refused him.

He hadn't considered that possibility until just now.

Fear gripped his heart.

The possibility of her completely dismissing him knotted his stomach, and he tamped down the urge to vomit right there in the bushes next to her gate. If she dismissed him completely, the magickal connection would snap and they would lose their chance to be mates.

"Perhaps sleep on it and we can talk again tomorrow?"

Her pulse slowed ever so slightly and she nodded.

Relief flowed over him like a tidal wave. At least she hadn't completely shut him down.

"Thank you."

"Good night." Her voice was soft, choked with churning emotions.

He knew this wasn't the right time to press. He'd take the small victory he'd been granted and look for her the next day.

Tonight she could be alone, though he doubted being alone was what she really desired at all. She was just too afraid to ask for more.

* * *

TEAGAN TRIED NOT to hurry as she opened the front door and slipped inside the small house she called home. It'd been a gift from the town, and she treasured its solitude above all else. No one had been invited inside since she arrived, and she had yet to raise the blinds or draw back the curtains even once.

It was a dark haven from the world around her.

But now the world was creeping in whether she wanted it to or not. The male she'd met this evening was a match, magickally speaking. He was a phenomenal Dom too, apparently, since he'd gotten her off more times in the space of an hour or so than Javier ever had in an entire evening session. Not that Javier's goal had ever been getting her off more than once. He was more of a build-it-up-and-keep-it-just-out-of-reach until the very end of the scene.

Still.

She didn't need a mate.

Didn't want a mate.

A new life wasn't something she deserved. Her husband

and daughter had been lost in the skirmish that ultimately had freed her from the Washington Republic and set her on the road to Sanctuary. She'd been given refuge. Food. A home. Clothing. Anything and everything she could possibly need—except her family. They'd been viciously shot down during the escape. She'd been shot too, but hadn't felt it until they got clear of the town. By then it was too late. She looked back over her shoulder and watched as WR soldiers executed both her husband and eight-year-old daughter.

If Travis and Garrett hadn't held her back, she would be lying dead next to her family. Most days she still thought that would've been the better alternative to the emotional hell she lived in now.

Mostly, when the pain got to be too much to bear, she begged Javier beat it out of her. After tonight with Finn, she wasn't sure that would work again. Finn had shown her another way. In the scene with him, she'd been completely focused on him. His touch. His hands. Her body had trembled with every caress.

But it wasn't right. She didn't deserve him, and he wouldn't want her after he knew a little more about her. Things were better the way they were. She just needed to get back to Javier and forget about Finn.

* * *

THE NEXT MORNING as she walked down the sidewalk toward Main Street Circle, she wasn't surprised when Javier appeared at her side from nowhere. They weren't exclusive, but she knew she was the only Lycan who played with him at the club.

He liked her in his own twisted way. Watched over her even.

That knowledge had kept her going when her mental capacity was at its lowest. Whether or not she was a true masochist, her sessions with Javier had kept her sane since losing her family. It had also kept her from ending her life on more than one occasion.

"How's my favorite bitch?" Javier slipped a familiar arm around her shoulder and pressed a kiss to her temple as he matched her walking pace with ease. He was about six foot two and built like a predatory cat, lean and mean—fangs to boot. "You seem thin, *mi dulce*," he purred, "Did you eat the food I put on your porch?"

Teagan nodded. "Most of it. Thank you. You know you don't have to feed me."

"I do. You don't take care of yourself. You'd be skin and bones if I didn't check up on you." He clucked his tongue when she opened her mouth to argue. "Don't deny it. You know I'm right."

Javier was probably the only soul in Sanctuary who knew what a mess she really was. He didn't judge her for it. Instead, he just let her figure out while being annoyingly helpful and much sweeter than she thought possible from a guy who enjoyed making her bleed and called her bitch or sweet in the same paragraph. She smiled.

His asshole behavior mixed with his out-of-character attentiveness always threw her off-kilter and helped wake her from the fog she usually existed in. He was so different from the other Protectors she'd met so far.

Erick and Bailey were nice enough. Eira was friends with the Drakonae and the Lycans from Ada, but she was still pretty normal as far as vampires went. She hadn't met the other Protector yet. There was at least one other male vampire she'd scented since moving to town.

"Come over to the cafe. The wolves have been raving about this week's menu being excellent."

"You don't eat. Why do you care?" Teagan asked, allowing a little bit of a teasing tone to sneak into her voice.

"I'd like to eat you," he answered, nuzzling her hair and nipping at her ear.

Feeding Javier was something she wished she could do. It seemed like such a small thing to offer him in exchange for the attention he gave her, but it went against her very nature. She'd grown up being taught not to feed a vampire, and she had no intention of breaking the vow she'd made to her pack years ago.

No Lycan willingly fed a vampire.

Ever.

It just wasn't done.

"I need to tell you something."

"Yes," he answered, stopping and turning her to face him.

"I scened with a Dom named Finn last night at Luck of the Draw." She swallowed a deep breath and looked up into the peaceful ice-blue eyes of the vampire she'd spent more time with than any other person in town since she'd arrived. He might be an asshole. But he was her asshole, and she trusted him to be honest with her. She owed him the same.

"Did Kylie match you?" His voice didn't waiver. In fact, his face showed no sign of surprise.

She'd showered thoroughly to make sure Finn's scent wasn't still on her. But Javier wore a look that said he'd already known.

Her head nodded of its own accord and she let her gaze fall to the ground.

"Did you like him, Teagan? It's okay if you did." He brushed his knuckles along her cheek.

"I don't know what to think. I need you to—"

32

"You don't need me. You hide with me." He cupped her chin and lifted her face to look up at him. "I give you what you want because you ask for it, but it's not what your soul wants." He pressed an accusatory finger to her collarbone. "At least I know if I'm the one hurting you, you won't hurt yourself. It's time for you to be with a man who can help you heal, *mi dulce*. If Finn is the right one, you should give him a chance. Kylie is never wrong. What did your magick say?"

Tears welled in her eyes, and her chest tightened like someone was squeezing it with a vise. It couldn't be. He was an asshole. He was supposed to tell her he wanted to keep her. That Finn couldn't have her. Not tell her to serve herself up on a silver platter to a man who might have a chance of actually touching her broken soul.

"I don't want another mate. I don't want to heal. You're supposed to be a jerk and punish me for even considering leaving you. I don't deserve... I—"

"Bitch, I like you too much to keep you from this opportunity. I'm not a Lycan, but as I understand it, Fate doesn't come calling often enough to ignore her," he rumbled, pulling her into a tight embrace. His arms wrapped around her, and she shuddered through the sobs that welled up and took hold.

CHAPTER 5

*F*inn ground his teeth together and strained to keep his fangs from descending. His wolf wanted to shred the vampire for touching Teagan the morning after.

He'd gone to try to coax the little female out of her house for breakfast at the café, but the vampire beat him to her. Teagan and Javier's scent led from a side street to Main Street Circle.

When he'd turned the corner and seen the vampire holding her in his arms, Finn had nearly lost it.

It wasn't his place. She wasn't his. Even though they were magickally compatible, it was all the female's choice. She had the final say, and apparently she was making her choice quite clearly. She wanted a man who hurt her and made her bleed, not someone who could see how much more she needed. How much more she would thrive on the attention he wanted to give her.

A growl rumbled in his throat just as he caught the last bit of their conversation. He'd just called Teagan a bitch and said something about fate. *What the fuck? He had no right to speak to her like that.*

He threw caution to the wind. Protector or not, he wasn't going to let Javier abuse her again. He approached them from downwind and was nearly on top of them before the vampire whirled with his mouth twisted into a snarl that Finn matched with his own vicious growl, fangs bared.

Javier shoved Teagan behind him protectively, and Finn took a step back. His behavior was unconscionable. This was a mistake. Teagan was a grown woman and a Lycan. He never should've threatened the man she chose to spend time with, even if that man was a blood-sucking, sadistic asshole.

Finn backed up another step. "I'm sorry, Teagan. I—" He turned and jogged down the street away from them. He didn't know what to say, but he'd probably ruined his only chance with her. The weight of that knowledge pressed down on his heart like a vise.

He'd waited decades to find a female who was magickally compatible. He wanted to have a true mate and experience love like his parents had. He wanted to have a family.

Teagan was the first woman he'd met in his entire eighty years of life that could offer him that and she... wasn't his and didn't want to be.

* * *

"You should go after him," Javier said, rubbing his chin, looking at her like she was a buffet of barbecue ribs. "I need to feed, and you need to talk to him."

"I'm a fucking mess, Javier. I don't belong with him. He wants the whole package. A mate. Probably babies. What am I supposed to say? I had those things and lost them. My heart shatters at the thought of having them again. I don't deserve it. I don't deserve him."

"That's where you're wrong, chica. You deserve to be happy again. This thing we do," he said, gesturing back and forth between them. "It's your way of punishing yourself and hiding from moving on with your life."

"Yours too," Teagan shot back, folding her arms across her chest. "Don't tell me you don't wish you could find someone to connect with."

He growled low in his chest. "You need to go to him," Javier answered, dodging her accusation. He turned and walked down the sidewalk, leaving her alone with her thoughts and frustrations.

She growled through a sigh. The vampire was a complete bastard and asshole, but he got her and he wasn't devoid of feelings. He knew why she did what she did, and he accepted her for it. He didn't judge or tell her she was wrong for seeking pain.

Not like Finn.

Javier didn't push her.

Until just now. And he'd pushed her away. Told her he wasn't what she needed. How dare he try to tell her what she did or didn't need? He was just a bloody vampire.

Except he was the only man she listened to.

Tears streamed down her cheeks. She stood in the early-morning breeze and sobbed alone. The only man who gave a damn about her in this town had just told her she needed to move on. Only she wasn't sure she was ready. Although her amount of readiness hadn't stopped the man she considered her Dom from shoving her down that path and away from him.

She took a few steps forward and turned down the street

Finn had taken. His smell lingered, and she drew in a deep breath of his warm spicy scent.

"Finn?" she whispered, hoping he might still be close enough to hear her.

Her tennis shoes patted softly against the pavement as she continued to walk, passing a few small shops before she entered one of the older Lycan neighborhoods in town.

The morning light bathed the old ranch-style homes in a soft glow. She could hear the inhabitants moving about inside, but no one was outdoors yet. They were all eating breakfast or drinking coffee. The scent of freshly ground beans drifted from nearly every house she passed.

She wasn't sure what she was looking for. Never having been to Finn's house, she didn't know where he lived. But his scent continued down the sidewalk, and so she kept following it.

There wasn't much else to do. She needed a Dom—a Master, actually. She needed the structure and security it gave her. Without Javier, she had nothing to keep her from sinking into oblivion again. Though she knew the vampire wouldn't ignore her completely, he'd made it clear in so many words that he was done being her Dom.

Finn's scent trailed down a walkway to a large one-story house. It was mixed with the scents of several other males who had recently come out into the front yard, though they'd since left. Anxiety fluttered in her heart like a wild bird trapped in a small cage.

"Finn?" she said aloud again.

The front door opened with a squeak and she jumped, biting her lip in the process. The coppery taste of her blood seeped slowly into her mouth and she grimaced.

Finn appeared in the doorway, all six and a half feet of solid muscle and primal hunger. He was shirtless and his body was slicked with sweat. She could smell the frustration hanging on him like a shroud. His desire peaked when their gazes met, his naturally brown eyes burned a bright yellow. His hands clenched at his sides, but he didn't approach. Nor did he move away. So maybe she still had a chance.

She wanted a chance.

Didn't she?

The magick between them was strong. The sense of belonging to him was too overwhelming to ignore, even through the pain of her memories. She needed him. But that need was also what completely terrified her. She didn't want to need someone that badly again. Loving another person meant opening herself up to loss, and she couldn't do that again.

Refused to do that again.

She listened hard. Though several male scents mixed with his in the yard and in the house, no one else was home. Finn's was the only heartbeat she heard. That knowledge relaxed her tensed muscles just slightly.

"You have to choose, Teagan. If you want Javier, I will leave you alone. I'll never bother you again." His voice broke on the last word, and his emotional declaration tugged at her walled-up heart.

He wasn't going to pressure her.

This choice was all hers to make.

"I... He said..." Her heart raced and words clogged her mouth like a stopped-up sink. What was she supposed to say? That she wanted more of what Finn had given her? That she had no one else to turn to because Javier was finished being her Master? That she needed another Master just to survive in life because she still woke in the middle of the night screaming? That she couldn't take care of herself because she was such a broken fucking mess?

She couldn't do this. She didn't want another mate. This would never work.

Turning around, she started down the walkway back to the street but was stopped by a hand on her shoulder.

"Don't leave." He was pushing the boundary of Lycan law. Accepting a mate was all the female's choice. Her choice. A male was not allowed to continue pursuing a female who had dismissed his advances.

His words were a command wrapped in a request.

Everything inside her wanted to lean into the strength of his voice, but she knew in the grand scheme of things he would hate her for what she couldn't give him. Yet there was that part of her that wanted desperately to belong to him. It was a primal need as much as an emotional one.

She wanted to submit and let someone else guide her through this life that had torn her soul to shreds.

CHAPTER 6

*M*aybe she could do this without giving him a piece of her heart. She could submit and follow his commands. She didn't have to accept him as a mate too, did she? They could just be Dom and submissive.

She turned again and faced him, dropping slowly to her knees there on the sidewalk. The act of surrendering just that simple thing released so much stress from her chest. She could breathe now. The choice had been made... at least for the present.

A slow sigh slipped from his body and he approached slowly, as if he was worried that any sudden movement might scare her away.

She placed her hands on her thighs the way Javier had taught her to start their sessions, presenting herself to her Dom. She dropped her eyes to the gray sidewalk and felt a shiver of excitement flutter down her spine when his bare feet came into view.

He touched her hair, sliding his fingers through the loose tresses. "Thank you. Come inside off the front lawn," he said, taking a step back and holding out a hand to help her up.

She slid her palm into his and felt the rush of their magickal connection sizzle between them. It was going to be hard not to give in to the mate call, but not impossible.

He walked toward his front door, pulling her along gently behind him. The scent of his roommates assailed her nostrils once the heavy front door closed behind them.

"They're in town. Won't be back for hours," he said, as if sensing exactly what was making her uneasy. "We have the house to ourselves. And I want to talk about a few rules for this relationship."

Rules? Relationship? That was fast.

"I want you as my sub, and I ask that you are exclusive with me. Do you agree?"

She glanced around the house, taking in the masculine leather furniture, dark hardwood floors, and broad walls painted a warm sandy-brown color. Anything to stall answering his question. She didn't want to agree right off the bat to being exclusive. What if last time had been a fluke? What if she hated him as a Dom? She wanted to be able to keep her options open.

"I'll consider it. When do I have to give you a definite answer?" she asked, hoping he wouldn't see straight through her stalling tactic.

His bright brown eyes flashed with a hint of irritation, but he merely smiled and shook his head. "Is a couple of days enough time?"

She swallowed and wiped her sweaty palms on the front of her pants. He'd gone for it. No argument at all. A quick nod answered his question and sealed her fate. She knew in the end she would choose to be exclusive with him, but it helped to feel like she had a little more control of the situation.

Even if she didn't.

He approached her again, and every nerve in her body stirred to life, anticipating where his fingers would touch. Her face? Her body? What did he want?

She knew he wanted her. The growing arousal behind his loose athletic shorts was more than obvious. Her face heated when she realized he'd caught her staring at his erection.

"Strip."

The single word echoed through the empty house and made her heart clench in her chest. She moved her hands to her waist and pushed her yoga pants to the floor, shaking her feet one at a time until her legs were free.

"Panties too."

She glanced up just in time to see him trace the edges of his lips with his tongue. His honey-brown eyes were beginning to glow yellow.

This was happening. They were going to have a scene right here in his home. And this time sex was happening. She knew it. He knew it.

It was an unspoken agreement.

Her sex pulsed with need as the rest of her tightened in anticipation of what was going to happen. Of what she wanted to happen.

She pulled her panties down and stepped out of them as well. Cool air flowed between her legs, chilling her damp sex. He hadn't even touched her yet and she felt as though she would come apart the second he did.

Straightening, she grabbed the hem of her shirt and pulled it off in one graceful movement, baring her breasts for his pleasure. Her nipples could've cut glass, and she wanted nothing more than his tongue to descend upon them and put her out of her misery.

She wanted him. Wanted more than pain. The realization ricocheted around in her mind like a pinball bent on hitting every single surface possible. Pain was what she deserved, not happiness. She'd let down the people most important in her life. Watched them die in front of her.

The memories flooded her vision and tears welled in her eyes. This wasn't what Finn wanted in a submissive. She had to keep this wrecked part of her to herself and take what he gave her while he was willing.

If she'd learned anything in life, it was that happiness was fleeting and only a second away from slipping out of grasp.

"Stay out of your head, Teagan. Focus just on this room. What you see. Smell. Feel."

He moved to stand behind her, sliding a hand to rest on the small curve of her lower back and the round top of her ass. Pushing ever so slightly, he walked her forward to the backside of the large brown couch in the living room. He took her clothes from her hand, folded and put them aside in a chair to his left, then returned to stand behind her.

"Lean forward over the couch."

His velvety voice slid over her skin like satin sheets.

She followed the command and lowered her torso forward until the upper half of her body lay over the couch back. The furniture was rounded and quite supportive, but the leather was cold at first, and she shivered as it adjusted to match her warm body temperature.

Finn's hands slid along her back and caressed her ass and thighs. His hands moved back to her hips, and he lifted her a few more inches, resting her body just high enough that her toes didn't touch the ground any longer.

"Close your eyes, keep your arms down in front of you. I'll be right back."

She did as she was told, digging her fingers into the cracks between the cushion she straddled and pressing her eyes tightly shut. Her sense of smell and hearing increased as her eyes closed and she listened to him leave the room, his footsteps soft on the floor as his bare feet padded in and out of several rooms. When he returned, she smelled the distinct scent of lube and vinyl. A thump at the base of the couch to her left was his way of letting her know they were going to use some toys.

She wanted to know what was in the bag, but at the same time the idea of not knowing was extremely exciting. Goose bumps had covered her from head to foot as she waited for the first touch. Strike. Slap. Caress.

Anything and everything he would give her. She wanted it all.

"Has anyone told you that you have a very pretty pussy?"

Warmth blazed through her body. What was he doing?

"I can't wait to put my cock deep inside that beautiful pussy." His fingers trailed over her ass, between her cheeks, and down her slick labia. "You want me there now don't you?" He slid two fingers inside and made a "come hither" motion.

Teagan moaned and clamped down on his hand, tightening her thighs around his wrist to hold his hand in place.

A sharp pop on the ass made her squeak and release his hand. "Greedy sub," he said, a hint of a smile in his tone. "You are allowed to come as often as you want until I say otherwise."

Teagan gulped. How many times was he planning on?

The sound of a zipper being pulled open caught her attention, and she listened as he dug around in the toy bag he'd brought out. A bottle cap popped open and she heard a gurgle as he squirted lube onto something.

"I know you think pain is the only way to escape whatever it is that you keep locked up in your head, but I'm going to show you another way."

Her vagina clenched in response to his words. It was a threat she desperately wanted him to follow through on.

Cold gel touched her, and she took a deep breath as he guided what felt like a huge silicone dildo toward the tight little ring of muscles that guarded her ass.

"Take another breath and push back. This is probably a little larger than you're used to, but I know you can manage it." His confidence in and expectation of her curbed a little of the panic she was feeling from the large malleable tip of what he was pressing against her ass.

She breathed in and out and did as he asked, pushing back against the slick toy. It breached the outer ring, which stretched her until she felt the sting of her body attempting to accommodate it. A few seconds later, the skin around her asshole and slit started to tingle. Even more blood rushed between her legs and she panted as her vagina began to convulse in time with each pulse of her heart. Her thighs flexed and she wanted him inside.

Right now.

She could do this. Anything he wanted as long as it was purely physical.

This could work.

CHAPTER 7

*H*er body trembled under his hands, but she responded to each command and didn't object as he filled her ass with a large dildo. What she didn't know yet was that it had a vibrator in it and he planned to make her come so hard and so many times this morning that she wouldn't be able to stand after they were finished. It would be a different kind of pain than what she was used to with Javier, but it would still hurt.

After the first four or five orgasms, she would be on the brink of begging him to stop, something he knew she never would do if he used a flogger or paddle to strike her.

She was conditioned to disconnect from her body when life became too much, and he needed that to change. Working through something was much healthier than hiding from it. He had an innate feeling that she held a lot more inside than one scene was going to uncover.

He pressed again, and the dildo slipped deep inside her ass, sliding up to the narrow neck and settling into place. She would have a hard time getting it out without his help, and that's exactly what he wanted. He pressed the button on the end of it and smiled as her entire body jerked against the vibrations. A low moan rolled from her chest, and he gave her ass a quick slap. She was so close, and that spark of fire from his palm should send her careening off the edge of the first cliff.

It did.

She writhed, moaning and biting back a scream of pleasure as an orgasm rolled through her body like a tidal wave set off by an underwater earthquake.

He slipped a hand between her legs and fondled her dripping vagina, pinching her clit slightly to make sure she stayed in the moment and didn't drift off too far in the sea of endorphins flooding her lymphatic system.

The sounds she made while trying to hold back made him even harder. He wanted nothing more than to strip and plunge deep inside her body, taking her fully and claiming her as his mate. But that wouldn't happen until she accepted him. Until she invited the claiming.

Lycan packs were ruled by an alpha pair. A female could rule alone for a while, but most packs wouldn't tolerate a single alpha for long. Balance was demanded. Males and females needed the connection to an alpha pair to solidify the hierarchy. Without the dual leadership, a pack would quickly splinter apart.

He left her side momentarily and reached into his toy bag again, pulling out a strappy piece of nylon that would hold a vibrator in place against her swollen clit.

"Take a deep breath." He soothed her, rubbing her lower back until the shuddering and moans died down to a more manageable level. It wouldn't be long before the next orgasm began coiling inside her.

He slipped the small straps of rubber beneath her pelvis and lifted her just enough to slide the vibrator pad into place over her mound and clit, then fastened the two straps around her waist and the other two around her thighs.

She was a good little sub. Not a hint of a question came from her lips, and her body relaxed the more he touched her. When the second vibrator came on though, she was going to come apart faster than she could imagine. He slipped his fingers between her legs again, loving how slick and needy she was for him. Withdrawing his fingers, he brought them to his lips and sucked the juice off them. She tasted like honey and sex.

His cock jerked inside his pants, and he bit the inside of his cheek to keep from groaning. Her scent and taste were heaven. He knew he'd never be able to get enough of her. If only he could convince her of the same.

Pressing the button tab on a string that trailed down from beneath her body, he smiled when her ass jerked into the air and a hiss slipped between her lips.

"Say thank you, Sir."

"Th-thank you, Sir," she gasped between pants, her entire lower body beginning to shudder as yet another orgasm coiled, readying to burst forth.

He pressed the tab again, raising the level of vibration another notch.

A moan started deep in her throat and then she tensed. Her toes curled and her knees pressed into the back of the couch, but no matter how she squirmed or wiggled, she couldn't get away from either toy. A raspy scream tore from her throat as she soared on her next high.

Another followed shortly after and then another, cascading through her body like waves crashing on a beach.

He stepped closer to her, settling his hips against the soft round globes of her ass. His dick prodded through his loose shorts.

"Please, Sir."

His heart tightened in his chest at the label she'd just bestowed. He hadn't asked her for that commitment, though he'd wanted to from the moment he played with her at the Castle.

"You want me, subbie?" He pulled his shorts down and prodded her slick entrance with his eager dick.

"Oh, yes. Please. Please. I need you inside me." She was panting again.

He slid a palm along her lower back. Her muscles were tightening, and she was squirming like a fish out of water. A smile played on his lips. He pressed the button on the end of the dildo in her ass and she moaned. The buzz from inside her picked up in intensity.

Placing his hands on either of her hips, he aligned himself with her gorgeous wet pussy and slid deep inside. She was so tight, and the vibrations from the toys attached to and inside of her only drove him into a harder state.

"Ah, ah." She started to scream and then muffled her voice against the couch cushions.

"I want to hear you, subbie. I want to hear every pant. Every moan. Every scream you can give me."

A half-growl-half-scream came from her throat, and Finn groaned as her pussy clenched down hard, milking his hard-on for everything it was worth. He pulled out and then slammed back, again and again, driving deep, working her into a frantic rhythm that left him sated and exhausted for the moment.

He pulled out slowly, stroking the quivering globes of her ass. Whimpers shuddered from her body as the vibrators mercilessly continued to stimulate her swollen bits.

A slow moan reverberated against the cushion of the leather couch, but she didn't beg him to make it stop. The orgasms now were going to wring her out like the squeegee attachment on a mop.

He smiled, massaging her ass and sliding his hand over the end of the dildo protruding from her tight little ass. He pressed the button again, raising the level of vibration and sending her careening over the cliff into yet another climax.

A scream echoed through the empty house, and her knees slammed into the back of the couch as her body tightened. He pressed down with his palm on the small of her back, keeping her grounded and in place over the back of the couch. She pushed back against the weight he pressed down with but still didn't ask to be released from the torture.

A sniffle and a sob gurgled up from the seat cushion where her face was buried. Her body shook from the occasional shudder as she came down from the last orgasm.

"Good girl, Teagan."

His dick was already hard again, but she wasn't ready for another round. She needed at least two more orgasms to reach the first breaking point, possibly three. The sobs were a good sign. But he needed her to find a way to use a safe word. If she'd come into this steeled against ever saying anything, it would take a lot to break through that wall, especially since he wasn't going to beat it out of her.

He slid his palm up and down the backs of her thighs, watching the muscles contract and release. Her toes flexed, and he slipped his hand between her legs, sliding two fingers into her wet vagina. He curved them just enough to rub against the front of her vaginal wall, and she shattered around him again.

A hard, raspy scream tore from her lungs, and her pussy clamped down on his fingers like a vise.

"Good subbie. Let it go," he coaxed. "Tell me when it's too

much. That's an order. Answer me so I know you understand."

"Y-yes, s-sir." Her voice was choppy and forced, but she got the words out clearly.

He used his other hand to find the control string hanging from the toy affixed to her clitoris. Clicking the button, he upped the speed by two levels and smiled when an angry hiss came from her mouth. "Don't you dare bite or claw my couch."

Her body shook as if the fury of a Texas tornado was corralled inside.

"Ahh. Ahhh." The moaning was louder now.

She wasn't getting much of a break between climaxes. It was amazing what the female body could endure. She had to be getting close to her breaking point. She couldn't just keep riding these orgasms without passing out. Eventually she'd safe-word.

Right?

CHAPTER 8

"*R*ed!" Her voice cried out, ragged and panting.

Finn moved at the speed of sound, flipping off the clitoral vibrator first and then turning off and removing the anal one. He unsnapped the straps secured around her thighs, lifted her limp lower body, and pulled the bright pink vibrator pad out from under her as well, dropping both toys into an empty bin to be cleaned and sanitized later.

"There you go. Good girl. I'm proud of you for using your safe word and recognizing when you'd had enough. That's good."

A rumbling growl from her chest was her only response.

It had taken longer than he'd thought it would for her to stop the vibrators. Five orgasms more than he'd predicted. She was one tough cookie... and in a lot of emotional pain to allow herself to go as far as she did.

He lifted her from the back of the couch, her body a limp dishrag in his arms, and pressed her tightly to his chest as he wrapped her in the soft fleece blanket he'd placed just to her right earlier in the session.

Walking with her around to the front of the couch, he sat at the end and cuddled her in his arms like a newborn. She was so petite. So vulnerable.

Her skin was cold and clammy, and a light sheen of sweat covered her forehead.

He reached to the table beside him and picked up the open bottle of water he'd brought from the kitchen earlier and set it to her lips, letting her take small sips, then broke off a piece of a chocolate bar and pressed it to her mouth. She opened for the chocolate, and he swore he saw just the slightest hint of a smile dance across her face before she ducked her head deeper into the folds of the blankets.

Her soft breath tickled his skin, and he listened as her heartbeat slowly returned to normal. Her breathing, too, evened out, and she was soon sleeping soundly on his chest, wrapped in his arms as if she belonged.

She did belong. She was his.

No other female Lycan in town was a perfect match. No other woman could give him the family he'd always wanted. For a century he'd waited and prayed. He'd gone out on missions for the town. Volunteered for rescue trips to help the pack up in Ada, Oklahoma, sneak out pockets of Lycans who'd been trapped in the intolerant republics of the former United States of America.

Nothing.

No one.

Not once in eighty years had he crossed paths with a single female that made his magick spark the way Teagan had the very second she'd walked into the Castle courtyard that night.

She was meant to be his, and he wouldn't let anyone or anything stand in his way. Especially not that bastard of a vampire, Javier. Or her misguided notion that she needed to be beaten and whipped to find pleasure.

Whatever it took, he would be the Dom she needed. The Master her soul desired.

* * *

HE HEARD his cousins on the porch before the door opened. Tightening his arms around the precious woman in his lap, he moved swiftly through the back of the house and into his bedroom, pushing the door closed behind him with his foot.

After tucking her into his big bed, he went into the bathroom and started a shower. He needed to clean up before she woke up and put on some clothes. He also needed to get his things from the living room and put them away. She would probably want her clothes back as well, but that could wait a few more minutes.

He listened as his cousins entered the house they all shared. A few muffled comments were exchanged, and then he heard the front door open and close again as they respectfully left him to finish what he'd started with Teagan.

They were good guys, his cousins. At first he'd been worried that four single Lycans living together would be a nightmare, but they'd grown closer as a family, and everyone was great about respecting each other's privacy.

The bar down the street was the perfect place to wait out anything. It was the only building in town with a functional radio and television. Even though the only thing anyone could watch was the news, it still provided a bit of interest from time to time. Electronics were banned in the town unless they'd been enchanted by one of the resident Bateman witches. Even though they lived in Texas, electronics could and still would be tracked by military and government.

Sanctuary needed to stay off the radar as much as possible. The lower the electromagnetic-frequency profile they could keep, the better for everyone. Satellites barely paid their little town any mind at all. And that's the way the town's founder, Rose Hilah, and everyone else wanted it to stay.

He rolled his neck as he stepped into the scalding spray of water. The shower door clicked shut behind him, and he let the stress of wondering how Teagan was going to react when she woke up slip away.

One step at a time.

For now he was satisfied that he'd gotten her to use a safe word. At least she wasn't so far gone that she couldn't feel anything any longer.

Hope bloomed in his heart and he grabbed hold of it.

* * *

TEAGAN OPENED her eyes and pulled back the edge of the dark blue fleece blanket that encapsulated her. The room was bright. White walls. Beige carpet. A dark-stained dresser matched the bed she was lying in. She sat up and shivered when a draft of chilly, air-conditioned air swept across her bare breast, making her nipples tighten instantly.

Where were her clothes?

Where was she?

Her body was sore in very nice places, and her clit ached from overuse. The memories came rushing back. Finn's couch. His hands. The toys he'd put on her. Used on her until she'd... safe-worded. Gods, she'd done it again! He hadn't even laid a hand on her. She'd been brought to rock bottom by a couple of fucking toys.

Not a whip.

Not a cane.

Two dumbass vibrators had done her in. This guy must think she was such a weakling.

Even so, she had to admit the sex had been amazing, but that's not what really stuck out in her mind. He'd held her after the whole thing was over. After she used her safe word. She'd never felt as close to another man as she had while she'd cuddled into Finn's big lap. He'd fed her chocolate and let her sip on a bottle of water until sheer exhaustion had claimed her.

She licked her lips. Remnants of the decadent chocolate still lingered.

Her body tingled from head to foot, and her muscles were like jelly, unable to contract and hold her upright without shaking. She pulled the blanket tighter around her naked body and let her bare feet touch the carpeted floor.

Water was running in the bathroom adjacent to the room. The door was slightly ajar, but she couldn't see him. His scent, however, permeated every molecule of air in the room. She took a deep breath and sighed.

The magick in her blood was excited by his scent. By his presence. He was a match to her magick like her previous husband had been. She'd known females who'd lived two hundred years before finding a compatible mate—now she'd found a second less than year after losing her beloved.

Tears welled in her eyes, burning as they cascaded down her cheeks. Her chest tightened, and she sucked in breath after breath. She needed to get out. To get away from this man. She didn't deserve him. She'd had her happiness. She'd had a wonderful mate and a beautiful daughter. She couldn't do it. What if she lost everything again?

It would kill her to go through it a second time.

If it hadn't been for Javier, the first time would've killed her several times over. Somehow he always knew when she was at her lowest and would show up. Probably had something to do with vampires having the ability to scent pheromones. Everyone in town might think he was an asshole without a heart, but that was the furthest thing from the truth.

He might be a sadist and get off on the pain of others, but he felt things deeply and valued her life. Even when she didn't value it at all.

Moving swiftly to the window, she unlatched the lock and shoved the frame up. She dropped the blanket to the floor and climbed out into the grass next to Finn's house. With a shudder, she shifted into her wolf form and took off across the front yard.

Hopefully Finn would just let her go. Javier had been wrong. She couldn't do this again. She couldn't let anyone else into what was left of her heart.

$\mathcal{F}$inn opened the door connecting the bathroom to his bedroom.

He knew before he saw the empty bed that she was gone.

His head turned as a breeze blew cool air across his wet chest. The window was open, and the blanket she'd been wrapped in was lying in a crumpled heap on the floor below it.

His lip curled and a growl simmered low in his gut. He hadn't thought she'd run, but he'd underestimated how hard she'd taken the scene... or how hard she would fight the connection between them.

He took a deep breath, scenting the salt from her tears on his sheets and the whiff of fur just outside the window where she'd shifted into wolf form to flee his house.

If a stronger hand was needed to keep her safe and centered, then that's exactly what she would get from him. They'd had sex. The bond had started.

He dressed quickly and left the house, headed toward Javier's place on the other side of town. The vampire had been her only confidant since she'd arrived in town. If anyone knew what made her tick, that asshole of a sadist would.

HE KNOCKED on the heavy oak door of Javier's brownstone. A second later the door opened, and he was face to face with the blue-eyed Spanish devil.

"Smells like it went well for you this morning," Javier drawled, his tone taking on the charm and confidence of a Southern-born aristocrat.

Finn snorted. He'd showered thoroughly, but even he could still smell Teagan. Their scents had started to mix. Eventually they would join permanently, marking each other as mates. Having sex with her had started the process, and there was nothing natural that could stop the magickal bond once it started.

"She ran," Finn said, crossing his arms over his chest and stepping away from the doorway. He turned and looked out across the street at a line of nearly identical brownstones. The Lycans in town called it vampire row. As much as the blood-suckers preferred their space and never shared territory except with vampires they considered mates, all the Protectors had elected to live in close proximity with each other, a phenomenon even Rose herself couldn't explain. He figured it was so they could keep an eye on each other.

"Of course she ran." Javier stepped out onto the porch, shutting his front door behind him. "You pushed her instead of punishing her."

"She doesn't need to be punished."

"How do you know?" Javier said, his voice dropping lower.

The hair on the back of Finn's neck rose, and he whirled back around to face the vampire. "What could she have possibly done to deserve your whipping her? She's not a masochist."

"I know."

The answer was so matter-of-fact. Javier knew she wasn't a masochist, and yet he'd agreed to top her and scene with her, knowing she wasn't sexually aroused by anything he was doing.

A growl started deep in his chest and rolled deeper until he could feel the tips of his fangs pressing against his lips uncomfortably.

The vampire responded in turn, flashing his fangs and allowing his eyes to swirl red for a brief moment.

"I protected her from herself, Finn. If not for me, the little wolf would've taken her life by now, several times over. So you can get all snarly if you want to, but it's not me you should be talking to." The male narrowed his gaze and Finn shifted uncomfortably on his feet.

The vampire's words were cold, but calculated and purposeful. He wasn't angry or defensive. He wasn't territorial or upset that Finn was Teagan's mate.

"It's her," Javier continued. "I told her to go to you. I told her I wouldn't be her Dom any longer. I told her not to ignore what Fate had brought her."

"What happened to her?"

"That's for her to say. Not me," Javier answered. "And you know it."

As much as he hated it, the bloodsucker was right. Teagan needed to be the one to tell him what'd happened in her past. She needed to accept him as a mate and a Dom. It wasn't common in Lycan culture for the male to push a female, but Finn could tell this was a special circumstance. This time tradition wouldn't serve Teagan well. For this once, he needed to push the choice for her own good.

If she hurt herself because he didn't know her past and couldn't protect her, he'd never forgive himself.

"Do you know where she might hide?"

"She won't hide, Lycan. She'll go look for another beating. It's the only way she knows to escape the pain."

"Will she come here?"

Javier shook his head. "She won't come back to me. Not after the way I ended things."

CHAPTER 10

inn pulled out the cell phone Meredith Bateman had enchanted for him and texted one of his cousins. If Javier was right, Teagan would show up at the Castle tonight looking to scene with the meanest Dom she could find.

If anyone fit that description, it was his cousin Brogan. The guy was as big as a house and had a scowl that could make the toughest badass sweaty and uncomfortable.

Meet me at the bar in an hour. -Finn

A text beeped through a few seconds later.

Sure man.

Finn opened the door to Riley's an hour later and walked into the dark room. Pool tables lined the far wall, surrounded by several of the leaders of the Sanctuary Lycan pack. This place was a mishmash of families, even though the hierarchy was the same as a family pack. There were dozens of family lines that called Sanctuary their home.

Pack structure here was handled more like an election than a right of bloodline as it was elsewhere, but it was a small price to pay for the freedom to raise your kids and live in a place that catered to Others and rarely saw the judgmental face of a human.

Lycans who called Sanctuary home would fight to the death to protect anyone who lived here, just as if they were pack themselves. Even though their species outnumbered all other supernaturals in the town, they were respectful to all and pulled their weight for the town's leader just like everyone else.

A good number of the residents raised livestock on land owned by the town. Others farmed. And still others ran a small fleet of supply trucks in and out of town. Finn was a deputy to the sheriff, a giant of a man who kept mostly to himself. He and four others who had lived in Sanctuary a long time helped police the growing population of Lycans.

His cousin Brogan was one of those other deputies.

The front door of Riley's slammed behind Finn, and Brogan turned his head to face him. The big man didn't smile, but Finn knew by the slightest twinkle in his eye that the wolf was curious.

"It's a bit early to be drinking, Finn." The corners of Brogan's lips twitched.

"I need a favor," Finn said, sliding onto the barstool next to his cousin.

Riley winked at him from behind the bar and slid a mug of ice water down the polished countertop.

Finn stopped the mug gently and tipped his head to the pretty redhead. Riley knew everything about nearly everyone in town. Her bar was gossip central, seconded only by Rose's

Cafe. Because Riley had the only TV and radio, she also had the scoop on what was happening outside Sanctuary—at least the government-slanted opinion they wanted the general population to know and believe.

* * *

TEAGAN WALKED into the crowded foyer of the Castle, warily checking for Finn. She hadn't seen him all day and hadn't noticed him anywhere near her house. Maybe he'd gotten the idea.

It wasn't like sneaking out of a guy's window was particularly subtle. For a Dom, he seemed to have taken it rather well.

Kylie caught her gaze and Teagan ducked through an open doorway. She didn't want to talk to the pixie and explain why she wasn't with the Dom Kylie's magick had said was a match.

She didn't want to talk to anyone. She didn't want to feel. Think.

Javier had practically dropped her on her ass. She'd run away from Finn. And now she had no one.

She padded through the courtyard, keeping her head down and catching quick glances of the Doms and subs moving through the open areas. Some were on their way to the rooms in the lower levels. Others were settling into the open playrooms on the ground floor.

Finn's scent was nowhere to be found, but instead of the knot of tension in her chest releasing, she found it tightening farther. She didn't want him, did she? *No.* She didn't want to feel. She wanted pain to drown out the torturous memories.

There had to be someone here who would give her that.

The hairs on the back of her neck stood on end. The

sense of being watched was overwhelming. She looked up, studying the people to her right and then to her left. When her gaze met his, her breath caught in her chest for a few seconds.

He was taller than Finn and built like an NFL player from back before the Riots. Back when life was simpler and the United States hadn't yet broken apart into five different dictatorships that called themselves Republics. But more than that, he looked terrifying. Which was exactly what she needed. She needed something to fear more than the memories that haunted her.

He whispered the word "Come," knowing full well she could hear him clearly even over the ambient noise of the people moving about the club, music on the overhead speakers, couples scening in the public rooms, and the laughter ringing out from the direction of the foyer.

She took a step toward him, a shiver passing down her spine. Even though she'd left things unsettled with Finn, he was going to be pissed as hell that she was approaching another Dom. He'd made it quite clear that he wanted an exclusive relationship.

Hell, they'd had sex too. She could feel the growing bond snaking its way through her heart, slowly taking hold, one tendril at a time, like a vine growing up the side of a naked stone wall.

She shook her head and took another step toward the giant Lycan. She didn't want a relationship. That was the whole reason she'd left Finn's house in a hurry. He wanted more than she could give, and he was just going to have to get over it.

She was the female. She got to decide. It was her right.

Taking a few more steps, she closed the remaining distance between herself and the large male. His scent was earthy and comforting, much like Finn's had been, though his presence and the scowl on his face said otherwise.

"What are you looking for, sub?"

"Pain," she answered, keeping direct eye contact. She wanted him to believe her. She wanted to believe it herself as well.

"Sex?" he asked, raising an inquisitive eyebrow.

She swallowed and nodded slowly.

"You don't seem sure about that."

Teagan squared her shoulders and breathed in deeply. "I'm sure."

He grunted, still appraising her with distrust. "Call me Sir. What's your name?"

"Teagan, Sir."

"We'll leave sex on the table for now and see how the scene goes. Restraints and flogging, perhaps a cane?"

"Yes, Sir." She watched him as he looked her up and down. There was attraction in his eyes, but also something else. Something she didn't recognize.

He gestured for her to follow but didn't make an attempt to touch her in any way. Not like Finn had insisted on doing.

It was better this way. Even with Javier's asshole attitude, she'd still gotten attached to him. The less physical contact, the better.

Every time Finn had touched her, she'd felt a rush from the magickal connection they shared. If this Dom wanted to keep his distance for now and his hands to himself, she was perfectly okay with that.

They moved through the open courtyard and into one of the open playrooms on the ground floor. There were several people standing around talking, but no one really paid attention as the man in front of her pulled two chains down from the ceiling rafters.

"Go get a set of padded cuffs from the wall and a blind-fold. Leave your clothes folded on the counter."

"Yes, Sir," she answered quickly, moving to the side of the room where a large wall and cabinet stood covered in toys, restraints, and other equipment. She slipped out of her camisole and yoga pants, folding and setting them on the counter as he'd requested. She was used to being naked in the club, but for some reason tonight it made her feel guilty. Like she was sharing a part of herself without permission.

It wasn't true though. Finn could say whatever he wanted, but she was the female. She had the final say on whether or not they became a bonded pair. He had to respect her choice.

She grabbed a set of two cuffs and then reached for a padded blindfold, but her hand hovered over it indecisively. Gulping a breath, she picked it up too and returned to the Lycan's side.

He took the cuffs, one at a time, and fastened them on her wrists.

"Yellow slows play and red stops it," he said, his voice smooth and deep, rolling over her frazzled nerves like molasses pouring from a jar.

"Yes, Sir."

"I have a friend coming in a few minutes. He wants to participate. Are you okay with that?"

Two guys. Since when did Lycans share? It was as uncommon as a blue moon unless the males were brothers and both magickally connected to the female. But if that's how this guy rolled, she didn't have much of a choice. She wanted the scene and no one else here tonight had taken an interest in her. Most seemed to already have a partner.

"Yes, Sir. I'm fine with that."

"Brave girl," he answered, placing the blindfold over her eyes. She shivered as his hands ran down each arm to the cuff, snapping them to the chains above her head. He pulled the chains taut until her arms were pulled out wider than her shoulders and she was just barely standing on the balls of her feet. If he'd pulled her much higher, she would've been on her tiptoes.

Darkness surrounded her, and she focused on her senses of smell and hearing. Footsteps lessened as people shuffled to find a place to watch the scene. Different scents filtered through from the crowd—Lycan, pixie, human.

"Do not speak from here on out unless it is to use a safe word or I ask you a direct question."

"Yes, Sir," she answered, taking a deep breath to prepare herself for the pain ahead. She dreaded and desired it at the same time. She knew it really wasn't what she wanted out of this power exchange, but it was a means to an end. And she desperately wanted to drop into that space where nothing mattered. Where she couldn't feel anything but the lashes of the whip or strikes of the cane. Where her body throbbed from the beating and buried the real reason she hurt.

His hand traced the curve of her breast and then his fingertips slid along her rib cage. The touch was light and tender, not what she was expecting from a man about to cane and flog her.

"You are beautiful, Teagan."

Her cheeks burned at the compliment, but when a familiar deep voice echoed the sentiment from across the room, her heart stopped for a brief moment. It was akin to being shot all over again.

Finn's scent filled her lungs as he walked closer, his footsteps light on the cool tile floor. She opened her mouth to speak but remembered her Dom's rules and pressed her lips tightly into a frown.

The whole thing was a setup. A trick. She didn't know it

for sure, but her gut said the two of them knew each other well... even though neither had spoken directly to each other yet.

Both of them circled her, their scents mixing together. Finn pressed the end of a cane to her stomach and tapped it lightly, sending a zing of desire straight to her core. On her back, the strips on a leather flogger teased the back of her thighs as the other Dom swung it back and forth, swishing it through the air. Each strike became harder, and her skin heated in response as the lashes alternately stung her thighs and her ass.

Distracting her from the *thwack* of the flogger, Finn tapped the cane up and down the front of her body, adding a harder sting here and there to keep her guessing.

The strikes came rhythmically to her backside. Only Finn kept changing the pace and where the cane fell. After a few minutes, it felt as though her skin was on fire. Every inch burned and tingled.

She shifted on her feet, feeling her consciousness start to drop into that blank space where she could feel what was happening but didn't care about it any longer.

On good sessions with Javier, she could spend an hour in that semiconscious state where the line between pleasure and pain ceased to exist altogether.

A harder *thwack* from the flogger pulled her forward again. Then an especially hard strike from the cane on her stomach brought out a hiss of breath.

She hadn't been ready for them to change pace.

"Brogan texted me. You know he was here at the club as bait for you," Finn whispered, his lips brushing against her ear sending a charge of magick rippling through her sensitive body. "You're mine, Teagan. Whatever it is that you need to work through, we will do it together."

Anger churned in her gut like a swamp full of gators fighting over a carcass. *How dare he.* It was her right to deny the match if she didn't want it. He had no place pushing it on her. The alphas wouldn't let it stand... except that she'd allowed a sexual encounter. Allowed the bond to start.

The intimacy at his house would be seen as her acceptance of the match. But even then, she still had the right to change her mind. She wasn't his until she said the words that finished the magickal bond that swirled and grew inside her heaving chest.

She mouthed the word "no," careful not to speak out loud.

CHAPTER 11

*N*o. Finn smiled at Teagan's attempt to speak without speaking. She was walking a fine line between following and disobeying Brogan's instructions. If his cousin had seen it, she wouldn't have gotten away with it. But Brogan wasn't facing the little wolf—he was.

Gods, she was beautiful and smelled like the best kind of sinful heaven. Even though she'd just told him "no," her arousal teased his nostrils like a fine wine that had been set out to breathe. He wanted to drink his fill now, but if he waited… it would be so much better.

He wanted her. He would have her. But it needed to be official. And she needed to be willing. She needed to want it as much as he did.

Finn splayed his palm over her stomach and drew in a deep draught of her scent. Magick surged between them, and he felt Teagan shudder. She felt it too, she just didn't want to. *Why? Why would she deny a match?*

Javier hadn't told him shit. But there was a lot more going on in her brain than she was letting anyone in on. No one else in town knew her story. Not even the alpha pair were privy. He'd asked.

He glanced back at the Lycan leaders standing to the edge of the room. Kate and Jackson O'Malley were the elected Lycan alpha leaders of Sanctuary. If anything arose in the Lycan community that they couldn't handle, Rose or the sheriff was brought in to settle it, but that hadn't occurred in years.

They'd come to the Castle tonight to make sure he didn't cross a line. Teagan's acceptance of their mate bond, though they'd agreed to him pushing her, had to be of her own free will. Kate had been very adamant that he would not have sex with Teagan again until she agreed to the pairing.

The fact that they had already been intimate had made the alpha female very uncomfortable. A child could already be involved, and Teagan would be shamed by the community for not accepting a Fated match after willingly having sex. Having a child was one of the gods' most treasured gifts in their community, something that not all Lycans were blessed to experience.

Running from Fate now would cost Teagan more than Finn was willing to let her pay.

Whatever her past was, they would get through it together. He wouldn't let her be cast out, and he wouldn't let her leave him. He needed her as much as he knew she wanted him. There was no denying the attraction between them.

There was something else keeping her from accepting a chance at happiness with him. Something dark and painful. Something she had shared with that blood-sucking vampire but wouldn't with anyone else.

He clenched his hand and released, taking in a deep breath of the citrus scent coming from her hair. Finn nodded to Brogan, and his cousin stepped away, placing the flogger on the counter across the room before leaving.

"I know you know I'm here, Teagan. I want you to know the alpha pair is here also to witness."

She jerked in the chains and growled but still didn't speak. She wanted her beating, and she was doing her best not to break the ground rules Brogan had laid out for the scene.

He tapped her stomach again with the cane in his hand and she panted, the scent of her arousal filling the air around her while at the same time he could see the visible tension in the muscles around her mouth. The tips of her fangs extended past the edge of her upper lip. With each strike, her lip curled, showing more and more of her bared fangs.

"Brogan left the room so we could work through—"

"I can't do this!" she snarled. "I left your house. I went looking for another Dom. Why would you still want me at all? I... I can't—" She shook the chains above her head but didn't ask to be freed.

His heart twisted in pain at her words. The cane he held slipped from his fingers and dropped to the floor with a soft tap that echoed through the still room.

No. She was wrong. He would show her she was wrong.

"Can't or won't? We have something between us that our people desire and treasure above anything else. A magickal connection. How can you just say no to that? Am I so terrible a man that I don't deserve a chance to win your heart?"

"No. That's not—" She stopped and lurched against the chains again. "Let me down. Now."

"Teagan, talk to me."

"No," she snarled. "Red! Let me down. Now. I won't let you keep me captive for this conversation. How dare you trick me? You both should be ashamed of yourselves." She yanked the chains again, baring her fangs at him. He could just imagine the angry yellow color her eyes probably were at this moment.

"You ran, Teagan. We started a bond and you ran. I merely chased." He approached, unbuckling her wrists one at a time.

She took a big step backward and tore the blindfold from her face. Her eyes weren't yellow anymore; in fact, they looked as if she would burst into tears at any moment.

"The only thing that can stop what we've started is a witch. You came here to try to drive me away. Well, it backfired and you're pissed. I get that. But you are mine, Teagan. I want you. All of you. Every single broken piece of your heart belongs to me."

"Fuck Fate!" she screamed, throwing the blindfold at his feet.

A growl started deep in his chest and Finn bared his fangs. "Kneel." His voice boomed through the room, bouncing off the stone floor and walls. In another life he would've been alpha in his family's pack. Here he was like everyone else. Bloodlines didn't mean anything in Sanctuary, but his bloodlines did give him an edge over the average Lycan.

If she truly didn't want him, she would be able to ignore his command. But if she felt the connection as strongly as he did, she wouldn't be able to overcome the need to follow her alpha. Her mate.

She stared at him. Seconds felt like hours.

Her fangs receded and she dropped to her knees. The second her hands touched the stone floor, sobs overwhelmed her and she crumpled into a fetal ball.

He started to move toward her but stopped himself and

turned toward Kate and Jackson. The alpha pair nodded their consent before turning to leave the room.

The bond had gone far enough to seal their fate. She was his and he was her alpha. Her Dom. The alpha pair would not go against his desire to take her officially as his mate. She had publicly submitted.

Turning back to Teagan, he closed the space between them in a few steps and scooped her naked, sobbing body into his arms.

One of the Sisters brought him a soft blanket. He whispered his thanks and wrapped his mate in the fleece before taking her out of the Castle. It only took him a few minutes to reach her front doorstep.

He tried the handle. *Locked.* He turned back and forth on her porch, looking for a place she would have a spare key. When he turned back to the door, he noticed a lip in the trim. Holding her tightly with one arm again, he felt along the top of the doorframe. His fingers brushed a loose piece of metal and he pulled a key down from the hiding place.

The door unlocked without complaint, and the magickal blue barrier flashed in the doorway like a shimmering liquid shield as he entered and closed the door behind him. The ward kept the Others known as Djinn from being able to teleport from outside buildings to the inside.

The inside of her house was Spartan but very clean. There was a small love seat and a lamp in the living room. He passed by the kitchen where a small table sat in a window nook with two wrought iron chairs. Turning down a dim hallway, he opened the first door and found her bedroom. A mattress lay on the floor, wrapped in pastel blue sheets, and a darker blue comforter lay scrunched to one side of the bed. Nothing else was in the room. No dresser or chest.

He set her gently on the edge of the mattress and then

headed back to her kitchen. She might think he was going to just tuck her in and leave, but that was not what she needed. She needed a Master. And he was beginning to realize just how badly.

Grabbing one of the dinette chairs, he returned to her bedroom and set the chair a few feet from her bed, facing her.

She lay on the mattress, watching him between the folds of the blanket, her sobs making her small frame shudder every few seconds.

CHAPTER 12

*W*hat did he think he was going to do? She didn't speak, instead just remained as silent as her body would allow. Eventually the sobbing would stop. She took a deep breath and tried to will the tears away.

What he'd done to her was humiliating and terrifying. They'd tricked her. Called the alphas in. And he'd showed his claim on her publicly. It would take an act of the gods to change their minds now. In their eyes, she was his mate. She'd accepted him the second her knees touched the cold stone floor of the Castle playroom.

But she had accepted him. If she had been able to ignore the command, he wouldn't be here. He would've left her alone. He wouldn't be laying claim to her broken heart.

It was broken. Shattered. There was nothing left to give another man. It didn't matter what stirrings she felt deep inside, she couldn't let him in. She couldn't let herself grow as close to him as she had to her precious Ethan.

"I deserve the truth, Teagan. No more running."

She met his piercing gaze and shivered. He was truly an alpha male. He might be mixed up in the hodgepodge of

Sanctuary now, but he'd come from royal bloodlines. He'd come from power.

"But first I will punish you for running from me yesterday."

Her chest tightened and she gasped for a breath. *Punish?* Her sex clenched as much in anticipation as it did in worry. He didn't like to hurt her. He'd already said as much on several occasions.

He patted his leg and motioned her forward. "Come lie over my lap."

She gulped air. Everything inside her screamed not to move, but she couldn't help but do what he wanted. That primal connection was stronger than any solitary will of her own. He was her Master.

She would be better with him than without him. Of that she was quite sure.

Climbing off the mattress, she moved on all fours to his side and carefully arranged herself over his strong thighs, ass up, bared and ready for the swats she knew were coming.

Her body trembled like a leaf in the wind, but at this moment in time, he didn't seem to care. His sympathy had been replaced by fierceness and a darkness she hadn't seen in him before.

"You ran from me. You allowed your fear to dictate your actions. You should've spoken to me about whatever was making you uncomfortable. That kind of behavior is unacceptable from here on out. Is that clear?"

* * *

"Yes, Master." Her answer was soft but clearly enunciated. And she'd used the term Master instead of Sir.

He took a deep breath and steadied his hand. He hated to

punish her, but she needed this from him as much as she didn't know she needed the tenderness.

"You will count to twenty-five. If you stop, we start over."

Her body tensed over his legs. He could hear her heart racing, but he could also smell her arousal. It bathed his senses in her delicious, sweet smell. He wanted nothing more than to forego this punishment and move on to taking her so completely that she never considered the possibility of her life being better anywhere but with him.

"Yes, Master."

He rubbed her bare ass and then raised his hand, bringing it down moments later with a hard *thwap* against her white skin.

The word "One" fell from her lips with a breathy gasp.

He raised his hand again and again, each swat bringing blood rushing to her skin. Her skin had shown an outline of his handprint after the first few, but now the whole of her cheeks were fiery red. His hand stung as well, but he didn't give her a break. If he did, she'd find her way into a place where the pain ceased to matter. He wanted it to matter. It needed to matter.

"Eigh...teen. Nine...teen," she counted out through clenched teeth.

Her tears wet the carpet below her head, but he continued.

He adjusted her body's angle over his lap and spread her legs so that the last few swats would be delivered against her ass and pussy.

"Twenty. Twenty-one!" She counted, but he could hear the pain in her voice and it tore a hole in his heart. " Twenty-two. Twenty-three. Twenty-f-four. Twenty-five." Her body shuddered from head to foot as she counted the last swat.

He held back a sigh of relief and flexed his hand. His palm was as cherry red as her ass and probably hurt just as much.

"Good girl." He gently caressed her burning skin. "Now we're going to fix the barrier between us. We can't be a strong pair unless we know the pain the other holds."

Her body continued to shudder from time to time with sobs, but they were starting to slow.

"I'll start by sharing something about myself. Then it will be your turn. If you don't want to share, you can choose to receive five more swats instead."

His lips curved into a grin at the small gasp that slipped between her lips.

"I lost my parents shortly after the Riots. They were amazing alphas and truly in love with each other. My brothers and cousins and I came to Sanctuary after being on the run constantly for years, even though I had to give up my birthright. This is my home, and I want you to feel the same way." He'd grown up in a loving home where his parents and aunts and uncles had been blessed to find their magickal mates. They all had children, most of whom he'd grown up with his whole life and several who had run with him from town to town after the Riots as they tried to make sense of the "new" world they found themselves wading through.

Her body shuddered in his lap. She was so small and so desperate for someone to take care of her. Why wouldn't she let him? He wanted to love and cherish her more than he'd wanted to do anything in years. She was the reason he hadn't taken up with any single females. She was the reason he hadn't given up on having a family. Fate surely wouldn't be so cruel as to finally give him a mate but then take her back because she didn't want a bond. He could sense she was fighting the attraction. Fighting everything about this match.

Why? Why didn't she want to be happy? A magickal mate was what every Lycan wished for... wasn't it?

Sure, plenty of them settled and gave up after a hundred years or so. But he never had. He couldn't. He'd known Fate would deliver the perfect woman. Now he just had to convince her of that truth as well.

"I don't deserve you, Finn. I don't deserve any of this."

"Why would you say that? You are a beautiful, strong, woman. Are you saying I don't deserve you?"

"I'm broken," she whispered, her breath a soft warm puff on his calf. "You deserve a woman who can love you back."

"You are attracted to me. That much is obvious. Getting to know each other is a process. I understand that." He wanted to beg and plead, but his pride wouldn't allow it. Still, he had to know why she wouldn't give him a chance. Who had hurt her so badly that she considered herself in such a terrible light? "What happened, Teagan? Tell me what broke you."

"I—" She started to speak but caught herself.

"You have two choices. Talk or get another five swats. Then we choose again."

His heart clenched when her naked body tensed across his thighs. The choice was there. She just had to make it.

"I watched my mate and daughter get executed and I did nothing."

His stomach dropped to the floor, and the air seemed to vanish from the room. Gods on earth and in heaven. No wonder she was in such a state. There was more to the story than she was letting on, but even her attachment to Javier made sense now. At least the blood-sucker hadn't left her alone to wallow in her misery.

He placed his hands on her shoulders and lifted her torso, lowering her to the floor so she could rest on her knees beside him. There would be no more punishments tonight. She'd finally told him what stood between them. Now he just had to find the right path for her to start healing. Pain was where she'd gone to hide from it before, so that was completely off the table.

"Teagan," he said, keeping his voice soft but firm. "I'm so sorry for your loss. I can't imagine the pain of losing someone you thought you would spend your entire life with. But take that feeling and apply it to my situation. Not only are you punishing yourself, you are denying me a chance with you. A chance to spend my life with the person that the universe has deemed perfect for me."

She lifted her head and met his gaze. Her tear-streaked cheeks and mussed-up hair didn't faze him at all. It was the tiny spark in her big brown eyes. Though small, it was a promise that she might be willing to try.

"I don't know how to move forward. Ethan would be so upset with me, but I just don't know how to function without him."

Hearing the other man's name on her lips shouldn't be painful, but a small corner of his heart would always be jealous that she'd already shared her love so completely with another man. He wanted that coveted place in her heart for himself, but it was important that he respect her previous mate's memory and that of her daughter. They would always deserve her love.

"First we are going to take a shower, and then you are going to get some sleep. Tomorrow we can discuss how we move forward from here. For now I want to officially request your submission to me as your Dom. I will care for you as long as I live, Teagan. Anything and everything you need will be my first thought when I rise and my last thought when I lie down next to you in the evening." He pulled a small black velvet bag from his jeans pocket and pulled out a thick silver chain. On the ring at the end hung a four-leaf clover and a heart charm.

Her eyes opened as wide as saucers, but she didn't run.

He drew in a slow breath. Her face was a rainbow of emotions from fear to excitement and back to reluctance again.

"I'm not asking for everything at once, Teagan. Just a chance to work toward what we could eventually be to each other. But no matter what, you are my sub and I am your Master in all things."

* * *

OFFERS DIDN'T GET MUCH BETTER than the one Finn was holding out in front of her. She wanted him as her Dom. Hell, she wanted him as more, but she just wasn't ready to admit it. Still, he was willing to take what she could give right now and wait patiently for the rest.

She was fooling herself if she thought her life would be better without Finn. Fate was giving her a second chance at a mate. Even more than that, he was a Dom who could help her navigate through the pain that tortured her soul. She didn't know him that well, but she knew in her heart he meant everything he said. He would be there for her. He would protect her from herself until she was able to stand on her own two feet.

The collar in his outstretched palm was beautiful. The chain was as thick around as her pinky finger and she found herself wondering what the weight of it around her neck would feel like. She wanted to know. Everything he'd said, she wanted.

"Yes," she said. "I can't promise much right now, but I can

promise to try." She drew her loose hair away from her bare shoulders and leaned forward, offering her neck.

The cool metal on her skin made her gasp, but after he'd clasped it and she dropped her hair back into place, she couldn't imagine ever taking it off. She touched the charms with the tips of her fingers and felt a sense of security surround her that she hadn't had since losing Ethan and Miranda.

Glancing up, she met Finn's gaze and reached forward, laying her hand on his knee. "Thank you."

One corner of his mouth twitched with just a hint of a smile. He was pleased. She had pleased him. After this whole ordeal, knowing that she had finally made a choice that made the man in front of her happy sent her heart flying. She wanted to see him smile again, and she wanted to be the reason he smiled every day. She wanted that for herself.

"Thank you," he answered, his big voice rumbling out and soothing her soul with those two simple words.

EPILOGUE

months later...

Teagan shuffled through the kitchen of the home she shared with Finn. Within hours of accepting his collar, he'd secured them a house together in the same neighborhood with his cousins but several doors down and on a secluded cul-de-sac so they could be as loud as they wanted. At least that's what he told her.

She smiled, bracing herself on the counter as she leaned down to retrieve a frying pan from the bottom cabinet. A few more weeks and she wouldn't be able to get that low without help. She needed to ask him to move some things around in the kitchen so she would still be able to get up and cook him breakfast without bothering him.

A punch to both her kidneys at the same time made her groan and drop the pan. Her hand flew to cradle her swollen belly, rubbing where one of the little feet had jabbed. She cringed at the racket as the pan crashed to the wooden floor. No way was she escaping this one unscathed.

"Teagan!" His voice bellowed through their home, filled with a terror that only a soon-to-be-father possessed.

She straightened up and waited, his footsteps pounding ever closer. His large form appeared around the corner. He was sopping wet and had forgotten to grab a towel on his way out of the shower. She couldn't help the smirk that curved her lips as her eyes were drawn to his bared family jewels.

"Good thing no one was here but me to witness your impressive entrance," she said, trying desperately to keep from snickering.

His eyes flew from her belly to the pan on the floor a few feet away and then met her gaze. The terror his voice had conveyed only moments ago fled his face and his brown eyes glowed bright yellow. He stalked toward her with that I-would-punish-you-if-you-weren't-pregnant look.

"It would be a shame to waste such an impressive entrance. Plus you owe me for scaring me."

Teagan threw on her best "shocked and appalled" face, but once he slid his hands over her shoulders and cupped one of her swollen breasts, her resolve melted. Her pussy was wet with need, and he was more than capable of providing relief.

"I do, Master," she purred, pushing her breast against his palm even harder.

"Breakfast can wait. And I don't want you bending over in the kitchen, love. Only on our bed." He turned her and scooped her up into his arms as if she weren't eight months pregnant. A few moments later, she was in bed with her Dom and breakfast was indeed forgotten as he carefully situated her on all fours, surrounded her with pillows, and then put his cock exactly where she hoped he would.

His palms splayed over her hips as he plunged deep, filling her completely.

She moaned as pleasure sparked through her entire body. Even her womb clamped down around her babies, holding them tight inside her she and Finn enjoyed their morning romp. It wasn't always instigated by crashing pans in the kitchen.

It didn't take much to convince him that she was needy. Teagan loved that he couldn't keep his hands off her. The pregnancy had been smooth sailing, and she'd been hornier than ever. In fact, the closer she came to her due date, the more wanton she became.

He slipped one of his hands around her hip and down between her legs, finding that perfect swollen little nub that begged so loudly for attention. His fingers circled it as he thrust, driving her higher and higher.

"Please," she gasped, her legs trembling from need.

"Please what?"

"Please, Master, make me come." The words slipped out as naturally as anything else she might say. The charms on her collar clinked together with each movement, reminding her of the covenant she'd made with this wonderful man. The promise and commitment had grown from Master and submissive to Master and now wife. They were less than a month away from welcoming their son and daughter into this world.

The pain that haunted her never truly disappeared, but with Finn she'd learned how to find joy in life again. Now she had a Master, a mate, a husband, and two babies on the way who needed a mother capable of laughter and happiness. Thanks to Finn, she was the person all three of them deserved.

* * *

I hope you enjoyed Mastered: Teagan!
Thank you for spending time with me in my world. Please
consider leaving a short review. Each one helps
tremendously.
XOXO
Krystal Shannan

Turn the page to read part of book 5, MY WARRIOR
WOLVES!

CHAPTER ONE

GARRETT

A HUFF ESCAPED from between my lips as I slid onto an
empty barstool at Riley's. The ache in my chest had turned
from an annoying throb to the pounding of a fatal wound. If
not for the Lycan moral code, I'd already be hauling ass up to
Ada to bring Charlie down to Sanctuary, kicking and
screaming if necessary. Her feelings on the matter could be
discussed later. She should be with us. Somehow, we had to
make her see that. Being away from her slowly ate away
pieces of my soul. The scent of her heat clung to my brother
and I. No amount of cold showers would relieve the need
that hardened my dick every time I thought about her, either.

I couldn't believe she'd sent Travis and I both away. We'd
risked our lives. Saved her from Xerxes' clutches in Savannah. Yet she'd sent us packing with no regard to the devel-
oping magickal bond torturing all three of us. There was no

way she wasn't hurting either. Once a mate bond started growing, only death would snap the connection.

My brother, Travis, sat next to me and waved to the tall redhead at the far end of the bar. Riley Moore acted as pack liaison between Rose, the town of Sanctuary's leader and founder, and the rest of the Lycans in town. It helped keep the peace, and most of us tried to avoid Rose anyway... except when the cafe served really good food. Which tended to be more often than not.

"What's happening, boys?" Riley asked, setting a pair of freshly filled beer steins in front of us. "You look like you swallowed a rattlesnake and it's trying to come back up, Garrett. What's eating you?"

"Nothing." I hoped she would accept the answer and just leave, but Riley didn't budge. In fact, she plopped her elbows on the bar and leaned forward, balancing her chin on her laced-together fingers.

"That's a bunch of bullshit." Her gaze flitted toward my brother. "You don't look much better, hon," she said to Travis. "I hear you left someone both of you want up in Ada."

"Who told you, Riley?"

"People talk," she said, winking. "This is a bar. Nothing stays secret for long when it stumbles in here."

I growled and took a long swig of the dark amber liquid in front of me. The rich brew hit just the right spot, and I closed my eyes for a second.

"Pretty good, right?" Riley asked. "One of the pixies over at the market grew me some extra special barley. This new recipe has been the favorite all week."

"It's really good," Travis answered before I could speak.

I nodded, agreeing with my older brother.

"I saw Eira's tattoo the other day. Gorgeous work as usual. Who wants to take credit?"

Travis shook his head.

I raised my mug and nodded. "That woman is something else. Despite how vampires normally react to silver, she barely flinched once from the silver needle."

"Probably has something to do with the fact that she's over a thousand years old and a Viking shield maiden." Riley tipped her head to the side. "She seems like a nice addition to the town, along with Killían. She's--what?--protector number six?"

"Yep."

"Y'all staying for the news brief at five? It's supposed to be from the SECR today. Not sure what those bastards have to share, but I've got to watch it anyway. Just in case there's something to report to Rose. The Sentinel never sleeps, you know."

"Nothing on the radio tonight?" Travis asked her, setting his half-empty beer stein on the countertop.

She shook her head. "Nope. Nothing scheduled."

I rotated the barstool until I could see the large screen TV she had on the wall just to our right.

She produced a remote control from beneath the bar and pressed a few buttons. The screen blared to life. News reporters stood in front of the federal building in downtown Savannah where Charlie said they'd been held in cages in the basement. The footage was old, at least several days. Politicians and the military fed exactly the information they wanted the people to see, but every once in a while, it did offer up something useful.

I half expected to see Xerxes on screen, but he wasn't that confident...or he just didn't have enough control of the SECR Republic yet to risk being exposed for the murdering bastard that he was.

Instead, a man with a teen girl standing just behind him

flashed across the screen for a moment. The male spouted some garbage about how the SECR no longer had to live in fear of Others. That they had purged their homeland and the creatures were gone.

The political bullshit didn't interest me, but the Asian-looking teenager standing behind the Mayor of Savannah did. Not unusual in and of herself, she looked eerily like the Kitsune woman who'd come back from Savannah with the rescue party only a short week ago. And she looked drugged –her body supported completely by a large bodyguard.

"Do you see what I do?" I whispered under my breath.

"Yep. Calling Mikjáll," Travis answered, pulling his cell phone from his pocket. "Take a pic when they show her face again."

I nodded and jumped up from the seat. Walking forward, I raised my cell and snapped a couple shots.

"They are on their way over."

"Who is it?" Riley asked. "You know that footage was taken several days ago, right?"

Nodding my head, I climbed back onto the barstool. "Yeah, I know. Not sure who she is exactly, but she looks too much like Riza to be a coincidence."

"The Kitsune female living with Mikjáll?"

"Yep. That would be her. That dragon barely leaves her and the baby's side." I turned back to the TV for a moment, but the Mayor was gone, and now some General prattled on about how new security measures were being implemented over the course of the next few weeks. Mostly just a bunch of bullshit that reminded people who lived in the SECR that it was illegal to own a firearm unless they were part of the Republic's military force.

Riza, barely five feet tall, came into the bar, followed closely by the seven-foot hulking Drakonae male. One wrong move on the dragon's part could send the fox shifter flying into the wall. For a man as big as Mikjáll, he managed to move with an unnatural fluidity.

He and Riza made an atypical match to say the least.

Riza should've been terrified of the angry dragon who'd come to Sanctuary having just lost his wife and his home. Instead, she'd latched onto him, and to everyone's surprise, he connected with her. They were inseparable. Both sympathetic to the other's losses.

I'd been worried about having Mikjáll on the mission to Savannah, but he'd proved he could keep his cool... for the most part. He had transformed into a fire-breathing dragon in the middle of a Savannah street, risking his species to exposure, but every single one of us knew we were alive because of that choice.

"Where is she?" Riza barreled straight toward the TV screen, but not seeing what she expected, she turned to my brother and me. "Mikjáll said you saw a girl who looked like me."

I pulled my phone from my pocket and swiped the screen until the picture I'd taken showed. She plucked the device from my hand and covered her mouth as a semi-hysterical sob escaped her lips.

"She's alive! I thought they killed her. We were captured together, but separated nearly a year ago. They told me she died."

"Who?" Mikjáll asked, stepping up to look at the picture. "Is she family?"

Riza nodded.

By this time, the entire bar had fallen into a hush. Even the Lycans in the back room playing pool had stilled.

"It's my sister. We were there together in Savannah. Djinn kidnapped us from our home. One day she became very ill, and they took her out of the facility where they were keeping me. The morning after they took her, one of the nurses told me Sochi died."

The tears streaming down the young woman's face made me wish I could disappear. "I shut down for months. I'm not even sure how long. They had to force feed me. They gave me shots, tried to artificially inseminate me at least four times before it finally took. Once I realized I was pregnant, I started eating again. I couldn't hurt her. But then as the pregnancy continued, I realized they meant to take the baby away from me."

"The next day, I used the powers I'd told them I didn't possess and slipped away while they were cleaning my room."

"How did you slip a guard?"

Riza's skin shimmered, and she literally disappeared from view. I could smell her presence. She hadn't left the room, but I couldn't see her. A second later, something glimmered a few feet away and she reappeared.

"Impressive," I said. "Wouldn't mind having that ability myself."

She nodded. "I wandered that facility for days after that, at term and miserable, scrimping and stealing food to stay alive. I birthed Suki in a closet and was nearly caught the next morning when I slept too long."

"Fuck!" Travis snarled, only to receive an angry glare from the hovering Drakonae.

"Several days later, I stumbled on the group of Lycans making their escape. I followed them out of the building and then met your rescue party. If Mikjáll hadn't grabbed me and Suki off the street that night, I don't know where we would be." She leaned into Mikjáll's large form, and the Drakonae wrapped an arm possessively around her shoulders. "We have to get her out of there. Now."

"We?" I asked, grimacing. "*We* barely made it out of Savannah alive the first time. What makes you think going back again will be any better? Plus, that video is a few days old. She might not be there anymore."

"I have to go back for her," Riza said, her eyes swirling with a mixture of pearlized colors. Sparks of electricity arced from her fingertips, a more offensive ability Kitsune possessed, and I couldn't help an instinctual flinch. No one ever wanted to be electrocuted. "Surely someone will help me. We can't just leave her there."

The appearance of the Kitsune's sister was likely a trap, but the pleading in her voice tugged at my heart, but the only person who might know a safe way in and out of the SECR didn't want to have anything to do with me or my brother. Charlie'd told us to leave. Even though the mate bond between us had started forming, we'd honored her wishes. The ball was in her court. We wouldn't approach her again unless she asked for us. It wasn't the Lycan way.

ABOUT THE AUTHOR

Krystal Shannan, also known as Emma Roman, lives in a sprawling ranch style home with her husband, daughter, and a pack of rescue Basset Hounds. She is an advocate for Autism Awareness and shares the experiences and adventures she's been through with her daughter whenever she can.

Needless to say, life is never boring when you have an elementary-aged special needs child you are homeschooling and half a dozen 4-legged friends roaming the house. They keep her and her husband busy, smiling, and laughing.

Krystal writes magick and Emma doesn't. If you are looking for leisurely-paced sweet romance, her books are probably not for you. However, for those looking for a story filled with adventure, passion, and just enough humor to make you laugh out loud. Welcome home!

Website | FaceBook | Twitter | GoodReads

Other Books By Krystal Shannan

Vegas Mates
Completed Series

Chasing Sam
Saving Margaret

Waking Sarah
Taking Nicole
Unwrapping Tess
Loving Hallie

Sanctuary, Texas
Completed Series

My Viking Vampire
My Dragon Masters
My Eternal Soldier
Mastered: Teagan
My Warrior Wolves
My Guardian Gryphon
My Vampire Knight

VonBrandt Family Pack
Part of the Somewhere, TX World

To Save A Mate
To Love A Mate
To Win A Mate
To Find A Mate

Moonbound is spinoff series from the VonBrandt Family
Pack…

MoonBound
Completed Series
Part of the Somewhere, TX World

The Werewolf Cowboy #1
The Werewolf Bodyguard #2

The Werewolf Ranger #3
Chasing A Wolf #4
Seducing A Wolf #5
Saving A Wolf #6
Broken Wolf #7
Hunted Wolf #8

Moonbound Box Set (#1-4)
Moonbound Box Set (#5-8)

Pool of Souls

Open House
Finding Hope

Contemporary Romance by Krystal's alter ego, Emma Roman.

Bad Boys, Billionaires & Bachelors

Can't Get You Off My Mind
What's Love Got To Do With It
You're The One That I Want
Accidentally In Love
Must Be Santa (Coming Next)

MacLaughlin Family
Completed Series

Trevor
Caiden
Harvey
Lizzy

CPSIA information can be obtained
at www.ICGtesting.com
Printed in the USA
FSHW02n1255190718
50695FS